Whatever After

DREAM ON

Whatever After

DREAM ON

SARAH MLYNOWSKI

 Scholastic Press/New York

Library of Congress Cataloging-in-Publication Data

Mlynowski, Sarah, author.

Dream on / Sarah Mlynowski. — First edition.

pages cm. — (Whatever after)

Summary: In this third adventure, Abby, her brother Jonah, and her friend Robin get sucked into the magic mirror and end up in the story of Sleeping Beauty, but when Robin pricks her finger and uses up the sleeping spell, Abby has to come up with a clever solution and a new happily-ever-after.

ISBN 978-0-545-41571-2

1. Sleeping Beauty (Tale) — Juvenile fiction. 2. Fairy tales. 3. Magic mirrors — Juvenile fiction. 4. Brothers and sisters — Juvenile fiction. [1. Fairy tales — Fiction. 2. Characters in literature — Fiction. 3. Magic — Fiction. 4. Brothers and sisters — Fiction.] I. Title. II. Series: Mlynowski, Sarah. Whatever after.

PZ7.M7135Dre 2014

813.6 — dc23

2013014463

12 11 10 9 8 7 6 5 4 3 2   14 15 16 17 18

Printed in the U.S.A.   40

First edition, January 2014

for my magical little family:
chloe-bear, anabellers, and papa.
you are a dream come true.

chapter one

There Is No Sleeping at a Sleepover

It's Saturday night and my new best friend, Robin, is sleeping over.

We're in the basement. She's teaching me a dance routine her older sister showed her. Right kick, left kick, arms up, turn! We're practicing in the mirror. We're getting very good.

I am having my very first sleepover since I moved to Smithville.

I have my very first Smithville best friend.

I actually have two Smithville best friends, Robin *and* Frankie. But I'm allowed to invite only one person to sleep over at a time since I have only one trundle bed. Also, according to Mom, two kids sleeping over is one too many. I'm going to have Frankie over next time.

I'm giddy. Which will make the "going to sleep" part of the sleepover a bit of a problem. But you're not really supposed to sleep at sleepovers, are you? You're supposed to stay up all night and whisper secrets. Also sneak into the kitchen and make s'mores if you have the ingredients, which I do. I bought them at the grocery store on Wednesday to prepare.

Anyway. There will be no sleeping at my sleepover. There will be only fun.

Suddenly, the lights in the basement flicker on and off.

"What is that?" Robin asks, looking around.

"I don't know," I say, getting a queasy feeling in my stomach. I shoot a nervous glance at the mirror. It's an antique, and about twice the size of me. The frame is made of stone and engraved with fairies and wands. Also, it's magic. (More on that in a sec.)

I hear my seven-year-old brother giggling from upstairs.

"Jonah!" I yell. "Stop playing with the lights!!"

The basement goes black.

"Turn that back on this second!" I holler. "Mooooooooom! Make him stop!"

The lights flick back on. There's more giggling.

"Sorry my brother is so annoying," I grumble.

Robin shrugs. "No prob. Little brothers are cute."

Only someone *without* a little brother would call little brothers cute.

Robin has a ridiculously COOL older sister named Dalia.

Dalia teaches Robin dance routines, lets her borrow her hoop earrings, and shows her how to apply green eye shadow. Dalia does not flicker the lights to annoy her sister.

"Where were we?" I ask, getting back into position. I catch our reflection in the mirror. Robin's hair is strawberry blonde and super curly. Dalia showed her how to scrunch it with gel. My brown hair is wavy and boring. Our pajamas are another example of the difference between us. Robin's wearing funky black pajama bottoms and a sparkly top (they're hand-me-downs from Dalia). My new pajamas are definitely cute — they have a dog paw-print pattern on them — but they look babyish next to Robin's.

Robin notices I'm staring at our reflection and waves. She's wearing pastel-green nail polish. "There's something odd about the mirror, don't you think?" she asks, touching the mirror's smooth glass.

"What do you mean?" I ask, even though I agree. OF COURSE I agree.

Here's what I can tell you about our mirror:

- A fairy named Maryrose lives inside it.
- When you knock three times on it, the mirror starts to swirl and hiss and turn purple.
- It slurps you up and takes you into a fairy tale.

Calling the mirror odd is a BIG understatement.

Robin wrinkles her nose. "It's like it's watching us. It's a haunted mirror!"

I force out a squeaky laugh, then try to change the subject. "Are you hungry? I'm starving. Let's go upstairs. Do you like s'mores?"

"Of course," she says. "Who doesn't like s'mores? But I just want to call my sister first to say hi." She picks her cell up off the desk.

Robin takes her phone everywhere she goes. It's decorated in yellow sparkles. She has unlimited texting. Only a few of the kids in our class have cells, so it's not like she can text everyone, but she can text some people.

I can't text anyone.

I can't decorate our technology with sparkles.

I can't call anyone.

Well, I can call people on our house line, but I can't call them when I'm on the go. I can't call them from the car. I can't call from school. I can't call from the park.

I have no cell phone.

I wish I had a cell phone.

Frankie doesn't have a cell phone, either, but that doesn't make me feel better. And unlike me she has two younger brothers. TWO! Can you imagine? Two Jonahs? I shudder.

Cell phone or no cell phone, there is NO WAY I'm letting Robin hang out in the basement without me. Too risky with my magic mirror.

"The reception is terrible down here," I lie. "Come upstairs." Actually, I have NO IDEA if it's a lie or not because I HAVE NO

CELL PHONE. She follows me upstairs and I show her to the living room to make her call. "I'll get started on the s'mores," I say. "Come when you're done."

"Where's Robin?" Mom asks when I reach the kitchen. She's unloading the dishwasher.

"She's making a call. On her *cell*."

Mom just smiles.

I sit on the kitchen table and swing my legs. "Can I have a cell phone?"

Mom laughs and puts away a stack of plates. "No way."

"But I need one," I explain.

"You don't need one," she says. "You want one."

"I want *and* need one."

"Why do you need one?"

"To text! To keep in touch! So you know where I am at all times!"

Mom smirks. "I know where you are at all times."

Clearly she doesn't know about the magic mirror in the basement. (Or the way it has swooped me to Floom, Mustard, and Zamel.)

"You'll get one —"

My heart leaps. "I will?"

"Yes. When you're older."

"Why can't I have one *now*?"

She puts away the coffee mugs. "Because you're too young. It's not necessary now. Be a kid for a bit. You have your whole life to be tethered to technology. You don't need to start in the fifth grade."

When she says the word *tethered* I can't help but imagine the game tetherball. My body is the pole, the string is my arm, and the ball is the cell phone. I would like to be tethered to a phone. As soon as possible. "When *can* I start?"

"We'll talk about it again when you're in middle school."

"Middle school is so far away. Like a hundred years away," I whine.

"Time goes fast," Mom says. "Just enjoy it. Now let's make s'mores."

Time does not go fast *enough*, if you ask me. It goes super-duper slow. It feels like I'm going to be a kid forever. I can't wait to be a grown-up. I have it all planned.

After elementary school I'll go to middle school, then high school, then college, then law school. Once I'm done with school, I'm going to be a lawyer and then I'm going to be a judge.

Judges definitely have their own cell phones.

I wonder if they text other judges when they're bored?

The s'mores are delicious. I make some for Jonah even though he asks if I can make his with ketchup. He's obsessed with ketchup. Obviously the answer to that is NO.

He eats them anyway, smacking his lips the whole time.

At nine thirty, Robin and I are in my room with the lights off. Robin is back on her phone. This time her mom called to say good night.

She's on her phone *a lot*. Which is totally understandable. If I had a cell phone, I'd be on it a lot, too.

"Yes, Mom," Robin says. She walks around the room as she chats. "Mom, it's *fine*." Pause. She stands by my dresser and fingers the rectangular jewelry box on my dresser. My *special* jewelry box.

Robin rolls her eyes. "I told her. I promise! Don't worry! Love you! Bye!"

She hangs up and tosses the phone into the orange leather satchel that has all her stuff in it. I know the bag used to be Dalia's.

"Everything okay?" I ask Robin. I really, really hope her mom didn't tell her she has to come home.

"All good," she says, and points to my jewelry box. "I love this."

I flush with pleasure. "Thanks. My nana gave it to me." My grandmother lives in Chicago and I miss her. I haven't seen her in months. I was supposed to visit her last weekend. I was going to fly BY MYSELF. But then there was a huge storm and all the airports were having delays and Mom was afraid I would get stranded somewhere, so I wasn't allowed to go.

Do you know what would make getting stranded in an airport easier? A cell phone.

But anyway. The fact that my nana gave me the jewelry box isn't the only thing that makes it special.

"Who are the people on the box?" Robin asks.

And there you go.

"They're fairy tale characters," I say.

She peers closer. "Oh, yeah, there's Sleeping Beauty sleeping, and Aladdin on a magic carpet. Is that Snow White? Why is she wearing pajamas?"

An excellent question.

Snow White *is* wearing pajamas on the jewelry box. Lime-green pajamas.

Specifically: *My* lime-green pajamas.

Why is Snow White wearing my lime-green pajamas?

She wasn't always dressed like that. Obviously. But Jonah and I changed the ending of Snow White's story when the mirror in our basement sucked us into her world.

All the fairy tale characters and their new endings appear on my jewelry box. And *only* on my jewelry box. Last week I flipped through the copy of *Fairy Tales* that we have in my school library — I mean media room, sorry — and the endings were the same as the originals.

But my jewelry box has the new endings.

I don't tell Robin about this, though. Jonah and I are not supposed to tell anyone.

Even though I really, really want to.

"I don't know why Snow White is wearing pajamas," I fib. "It's silly, I guess."

Then I yawn. I don't mean to. I want to stay up all night and keep talking.

Then Robin yawns. Which is not surprising because yawns are contagious.

She crawls into the trundle bed.

"Why don't we just close our eyes for a sec?" I ask. "Then we'll keep talking."

"Okay," Robin says. "Just for a sec."

We'll take a quick nap. And then we'll have fun. So much fun. And more s'mores — I close my eyes — but not s'mores with ketchup.

✳ chapter two ✳

Wide Awake

I'm woken up by a loud creak.

I jump up in bed.

I twist to look at my alarm clock—it's eleven fifty-five at night. Crumbs. We weren't supposed to sleep for that long. We were just supposed to take a catnap!

I hear another creak. I look over at the trundle bed to see if Robin is still sleeping.

The trundle is bed is empty.

Huh?

Where is she?

I didn't imagine the sleepover, did I? Was it a dream? Was Robin really here?

I spot her orange leather bag on the floor.

Nope, she definitely *was* here and still is. But where?

Maybe she's hiding somewhere under the blankets? Jonah always used to hide under blankets during games of hide-and-seek. I jump out of my bed and toss her covers onto the floor.

Nope. No Robin.

Hmm.

Oh! My door is wide open. I definitely closed it before we went to sleep. Robin must be in the bathroom. I'm sure she'll be back any minute.

I'll just wait.

I sit on the edge of my bed.

I twiddle my thumbs.

And wait.

Still waiting.

She is taking an awful long time in the bathroom. I should make sure she's okay. I tiptoe out into the hall. The bathroom door is open and the light is off. She is not in the bathroom.

"Robin?" I whisper.

There's no answer.

"Robin!" I whisper again, although this time it's a little louder and not really a whisper.

Jonah's door flies opens. "Did you call me?" He's wearing Superman pajamas and holding some sort of electronic game in his hand.

"No," I tell him. "What are you doing up?"

"I was playing Karate Crocs. It's a new game about crocodiles that do karate." *CREAK*. "Did you hear that?" Jonah asks me, looking down the stairs. "That came from the basement."

It *did* sound like it came from the basement.

"I can't find Robin," I tell him. Could Robin be in the basement?

CREAK. That also came from the basement.

Why would Robin be in the basement? She wouldn't be! She's not in the basement! Then why am I starting to panic?

"I think she's in the basement," Jonah says.

Great.

I carefully climb down the two flights of stairs with Jonah close behind me.

When I open the basement door I hear another creak.

"Robin?" I call out. "Are you there?"

I hurry down the steps and spot her right away. She's walking around the room in her pajamas with a glazed expression on her face.

"Robin, is everything okay?" I ask. "What are you doing? Did you forget something down here?"

She doesn't answer. She just continues walking in a circle.

"Is she sleepwalking?" I wonder out loud.

Jonah rubs his eyes with the back of his hand. "Don't sleepwalkers keep their arms out? Like zombies? Maybe she's a zombie."

"Robin is not a zombie," I say. Though she does look a bit like a zombie.

"Maybe she turns into a zombie only at night," Jonah says. "And that's why you never knew."

"She does *not* turn into a zombie at night!" I insist. Still, shivers spread from my back to my fingers. "Robin, you're creeping us out! Talk to me!"

Instead of answering, Robin bumps right into the mirror.

The magic mirror.

I hear a low hissing sound. *Sssssssssss.*

Oh no oh no oh no. The mirror is waking up.

Robin takes a step back.

I reach for her even though she's freaking me out. But it's too late.

She bumps into the mirror again.

My whole body tenses as a warm purple light radiates from the mirror. If Robin hits the mirror one more time, it is going to suck her up and take her into a fairy tale. I CANNOT let that happen. I have to stop it!

"Maryrose, are you there?" I cry. "Are you listening? Please don't take my new best friend! STOP, ROBIN, STOP!"

I reach out to grab on to her again, but she steps forward and out of my grasp. It's too late.

Robin bumps into the mirror a third time.

First her reflection starts to swirl like it's been caught in a washing machine.

No, no, no!

Then the mirror turns into a vacuum, pulling Robin toward it. Finally, I manage to get a grip on her wrist.

"No! Don't go!" I shout. I feel like I can't breathe.

Jonah is holding on to the banister. I grab on to him with one hand, and on to Robin's wrist with the other. But it's like I'm playing tug-of-war and losing. Robin's right foot disappears inside the mirror first. Then her whole leg. Then half her face disappears inside.

It's too hard to hold on! I let go of her wrist, and the rest of Robin gets slurped by the mirror.

Getting my best friend swallowed into a fairy tale was so NOT part of my sleepover plan.

"Come on," I urge Jonah. "We have to go, too. We can't leave her alone in there. She's not even awake!"

Not that we have a choice. The mirror is already tugging us by our socks.

Speaking of socks, Jonah's have holes in them. I can see both his big toes. Why hasn't he thrown those out?

"Awesome! Let's go!" my brother calls out. His eyes are lit up with excitement. Unlike me, Jonah is always up for an adventure. But normally I'm excited about going into the mirror, too. I want to see more of the stories come to life. I want to find out the truth about Maryrose. Just not TONIGHT. It's sleepover night!

Robin will never be allowed to come over again if she's poisoned by a witch or turned into a mouse while she's visiting my house.

"Where do you think we're gonna go?" Jonah asks. "*Jack and the Beanstalk?*"

"Why do you always think we're going to *Jack and the Beanstalk?*"

"Don't you want to meet a giant?" he asks, and lets go of the banister.

Before I can tell him that no, I do not, the mirror gives us a massive tug and we both get sucked inside.

✳ chapter three ✳

These Socks Are Made for Walking

going through the mirror never hurts. It feels like you're
walking through air or an open door.

When we find our balance we realize we're on the ground
floor of a stone tower. There's a spiral staircase that starts beside
us and winds its way up and around the inside of the tower for at
least fifteen flights, maybe more. There are a few round windows
letting sunlight stream in.

On the floor there are piles and piles of copper pots, different
sized plates, drinking glasses, and cutlery. So. Many. Piles. It's
like we're in a garage where people keep their extra stuff.

It's damp in here, like a bathroom after a shower. And it smells sweet and kind of floral. Like the time Jonah dropped Mom's perfume bottle on the floor. Mom was not happy.

"What fairy tale are we in?" Jonah asks me.

Hmm. We're in a tower . . . which fairy tale is in a tower? Oh! "I bet we're in *Rapunzel*!"

I spot Robin standing on the other side of the room. Her arms are by her side and she's blinking, clearly confused.

"Are you okay?" I ask her.

"Abby? Am I dreaming?" she asks.

"Not exactly," I say.

"Where are we?"

"Um, it's kind of a funny story." I stall. I guess I have to explain.

"I woke up and you weren't in your bed," I tell her. "We followed you to the basement and —"

"I thought you were a zombie," Jonah says, holding his arms out rigidly. "It was awesome."

Robin covers her face with her hands and groans. "I can't believe I sleepwalked!"

I was right! She *was* sleepwalking.

"You sleepwalked all the way down two flights of stairs?" I cry. "Isn't that dangerous?"

"Yes! I haven't done it in years," she explains. "My mom would never have let me sleep over if she thought I was still doing it . . . and I promised her that I told you and your mom just in case. This is so embarrassing." She looks around. "But where are we? Is this a room in your house?"

"No. See, when you went into our basement, you —"

"I wonder where those stairs go," Jonah remarks, cutting me off and running to the first step.

"Wait, Jonah, hold on!" I call out. "We need a plan! We don't want to scare Rapunzel!"

"We don't know for sure we're in *Rapunzel*!" he says, already climbing. "Maybe it's *Jack and the Beanstalk*!"

My brother is obsessed.

"No. I'm pretty sure it's *Rapunzel*!" I call. But Robin is on Jonah's heels, and they are already a few flights up. "Where are you going?" I yell.

"To the top!" they both shout back. You'd think Robin and Jonah were the ones related.

"I'm coming! Be careful!" I've just realized that the stairs have no railing. I follow my brother and Robin up anyway.

So. Many. Stairs. They're stone and partly worn away. I bet they'd hurt to fall on. Good thing Robin isn't still sleepwalking.

"Don't say anything to Rapunzel until I get there!" I call up to Jonah. I steady myself against the wall.

"Who's Rapunzel again?" Jonah asks.

"The one with the long hair. She hangs it out the side window and the prince climbs it like a ladder!" My nana used to read the fairy tales to both Jonah and me when we were younger. I paid attention 95 percent of the time. My brother paid attention 5 percent of the time.

"I don't understand," Robin says. "What does this have to do with Rapunzel?"

"That's what I was trying to explain," I huff as I continue to climb. "You see, we have this mirror in our basement, and this fairy, Maryrose, she kind of —"

"Someone named Maryrose lives in your basement?" Robin asks.

"Well, sort of." Huff, huff. I can't talk and climb at the same timc. "I'll explain when we get there," I say, even though I am not entirely sure where *there* is.

It's getting hot. This place could really use an air conditioner.

"'Kay!" Robin calls. "I'm almost at the top!"

"Be careful!" I warn. I've been through the mirror three times already, so I know the drill. But Robin is a novice.

"Hello," I hear Robin say in a friendly voice as she reaches the last stair and disappears from view.

Where did she go? Who is she talking to?

"Who is she saying hello to?" I ask Jonah, since he's closer to the threshold than I am. "Who's there?"

"I don't know yet," he replies, and then he disappears from view, too. "What's that?" I hear him ask.

What's what? Argh! I need to know what's going on. I push myself up the last few stairs until I'm finally — huff, huff — at the top.

I step into a bright attic. There's a small cot covered in a lumpy blanket near the wall. It actually looks more like a burlap sack than a blanket—I feel bad for whoever has to sleep there. Above me, there's a large skylight in the low ceiling, and the sun is pouring in. In the back of the room a woman is sitting on a bench in front of some sort of contraption. It looks a little like a violin. It has a bunch of strings. And a wheel.

The woman is wearing black pants and a loose black blouse. She looks about Mom's age — no, older than Mom. But younger than Nana. Her hair is a mix of blond and gray and is cut short. She is definitely *not* Rapunzel. She's smiling, but her eyes look flat and dull.

I join Robin and Jonah in the center of the room.

"Which one of you is the princess?" the woman asks. Her fake smile broadens. It looks less natural the wider it gets, like when the wolf smiles in *Little Red Riding Hood*.

We're not in *Little Red Riding Hood*, are we?

No. I don't see any fangs. Or fur.

"Neither of us is a princess." I'm careful to keep my tone even. I wish I knew whether this woman was a nice character or a villain. My mind races. I guess I could just ask her. "What's your name?"

The woman glares at us. "What's *your* name?" she barks back.

Her very bad manners point to villain. I put my arm around Jonah.

"I'm Robin, and this is Abby and Jonah," Robin says, her voice bouncy. She's still excited about being in a strange tower, I guess.

The woman looks back and forth between us, clearly confused about what to do. Her confusion makes me relax a little, because villains usually have a clear idea of their own sinister plans.

"I'm . . . Lottie," she finally says.

I think back to all the fairy tales my nana used to read me. I don't remember any Lottie. But sometimes the characters' names are different in real life — make that mirror life — than they are in the original stories.

Robin points to the violin-like contraption. "What is that?"

Is it a harp? A cello? A wheelbarrow?

Why is it glowing?

All those threads . . . Is it making a scarf? Is it a sewing machine? What's that pointy part that looks like a needle?

Sewing . . . needles . . .

"Oh! Oh! Oh!" I shriek. "We're in *Sleeping Beauty*!"

Yes! The contraption is one of those old-fashioned spinning

wheels! It makes yarn or threads or something like that. This is definitely Sleeping Beauty's fairy tale. Hurray! I love that story.

Robin is walking toward the sewing contraption.

"Robin," I say.

She keeps walking. She does not notice my warning tone.

"Robin, stop!" I yell.

She spins around and bumps the back of her arm into the pointy part. It pricks her right in the elbow.

She grimaces.

I cringe. "Are you okay?" I have a bad feeling about this.

"That stung," Robin says. She yawns. "I think it's bleeding. What time is it? It's so bright in here. Why am I so tired?"

Oh, no.

If she's tired that could mean . . .

Robin spots the cot and stumbles toward it. She kind of trips over the edge and flops onto her back. "I'm going to take a nap," she mumbles, her eyes already half shut.

Within a second her eyes are closed completely and she's breathing heavily. She's fast asleep.

In the story of *Sleeping Beauty*, the princess pricks her finger and falls asleep for a hundred years.

Now Robin pricked her elbow and fell asleep on a lumpy burlap sack.

Oh my goodness. My heart pounds against my chest. This is bad. Really bad.

Ladies and gentlemen, I am pretty sure Robin just pricked herself right into a sleeping spell.

✳ chapter four ✳

Sleepyhead

I squeeze Robin's hands again and again. "Robin, wake up! You have to wake up!" I whimper.

Her eyelids don't even flicker. Robin is out cold.

Lottie frowns. "Her fault. She should have been more careful."

I can't help but agree.

"What's going on?" Jonah asks, chewing his bottom lip. "Why is she asleep? Where are we?"

I keep hand-squeezing as I answer. "We're in the story of *Sleeping Beauty*. And Robin pricked herself on the pointy part of the sewing contraption! And she's, obviously, sound asleep."

"Does that mean we messed up the story?" Jonah asks.

"I don't know," I snap. Just because Jonah didn't pay attention to our nana's stories doesn't mean I should have to explain everything to him all the time. "Let's try and wake her up. ROBIN, WAKE UP!" I yell again, an inch from her face.

"You two better be quiet," Lottie snaps. "The princess is about to come in here and she needs to prick her finger."

I ball my hands into fists. "We need to help our friend! Do you know how to wake her up?"

"She's not my problem," Lottie retorts. "And you need to get out of the way."

"We're not going anywhere," I insist, putting my fists on my hips. No way am I leaving Robin.

"Then you better hide so the princess doesn't see you. And be quiet!"

I grab Jonah by the hand and we crouch between the curved wall and the bed.

"Who's Lottie?" he asks.

Who *is* Lottie? "If we're in *Sleeping Beauty* and Lottie is a villain, then she is probably . . . the evil fairy?!" I squeeze my brother's hand. This could be dangerous.

"What makes the evil fairy evil?" my brother asks. "Can you tell me the whole story, please?"

I sigh. "Okay. A king and queen were having trouble having a baby. But eventually a princess was born. They invited twelve fairies to a party to celebrate her birth. All the fairies in the kingdom except for one."

He shakes his head solemnly. "That wasn't very nice."

"It certainly wasn't," Lottie pipes in. "In fact, it's *extremely* rude. And hurtful."

Jonah nods in agreement. "At school you can't just leave one kid off your birthday list. You have to invite the whole class."

Lottie squares her shoulders. "That is a *very* good rule."

"They didn't invite her because they had only twelve sets of gold plates instead of thirteen," I say. "I don't know why they couldn't just use paper plates. But anyway, each fairy gave the princess a magical gift."

Jonah's eyes widen. "Like what? Real crocodiles that know karate?"

I snort. "No. Useful things like courage and kindness. Intelligence and beauty. The ability to play the piano."

"I can already play the piano," Jonah remarks.

" 'Chopsticks' docs not count," I counter.

He juts out his chin. "Does so."

"Enough," Lottie says. "You guys are way too loud."

I tell the rest of the story in whispers close to Jonah's ear so Lottie can't hear.

"The eleventh fairy had just given her gift when the thirteenth fairy — Lottie, I guess — stormed into the party all mad at being overlooked. She said she had a gift for the princess: When the princess turned fifteen, she'd prick her finger on a spindle . . . and die." I pause, realizing something. "Oh. Right. That's what the pointy part is called. The spindle."

"That's the worst birthday present ever," Jonah whispers. His breath smells like marshmallows. Did he not brush his teeth after the s'mores? Apparently my brother needs a lesson on proper dental hygiene. Where was I? Oh, right.

"Luckily, the twelfth fairy hadn't had her turn yet. She said she couldn't undo the older fairy's spell — the thirteenth fairy was really old and powerful — but she could soften it. She said that instead of dying when she pricked herself, the princess would fall into a deep sleep. After a hundred years, a prince would wake her up. The king and queen still didn't want that to happen, though. So they banned all spindles from the kingdom."

"Not all of them." Jonah motions to the one in front of us.

"Good point," I whisper back. Then I try to stretch my legs. My feet are tingling. "Seems like this one slipped through their fingers. Anyway. One day when Sleeping Beauty was fifteen, she was exploring the palace. She went into a tower and saw the spindle. She pricked her finger by accident and fell into a deep sleep, and everyone in the castle fell asleep, too. No one took care of the palace and it became overgrown with vines and leaves. A hundred years later a prince cut through them all and found Sleeping Beauty. He kissed her and woke her up. Everyone else in the family woke up, too. And they lived —"

"Happily ever after," Jonah said. "I figured. So what do you think is going to happen next? Is Sleeping Beauty going to show up now and accidentally prick her finger and then fall asleep next to Robin? The bed is pretty small."

"I guess so."

Clomp, clomp, clomp.

Lottie perks up.

"Someone's coming up thc stairs!" Jonah exclaims.

"SHHHH!" Lottie hisses in our direction.

"So what do we do?" Jonah asks. "Do we let her prick her finger like she's supposed to?"

"I guess so," I say. "She gets a happy ending. Might as well leave it as it is."

Clomp, clomp, clomp!

Jonah and I both duck.

The door is thrown open and a teenage girl bursts into the room. She has straight blond hair, pale skin, pink cheeks, and big blue eyes. She's tall but delicate looking. She looks a lot like the Sleeping Beauty on my jewelry box, except here she's awake. She's wearing a red dress cinched at the waist with a sparkly gold sash. She's also wearing a gold crown. She has a determined look on her face.

"Hello!" Lottie says to the princess super-casually. Her pretend smile returns, looking just as fake as it did before. "You must be the princess. Come on in."

Any second now, the princess is going to approach the spindle and accidentally prick her finger. Then the story can go on the way it's supposed to. We'll just have to figure out how to wake up Robin.

The princess opens her mouth to speak.

I expect her to say something like "Oh! What could that be?" or "I've never seen that before. Maybe I should touch it!"

But instead she says, "Finally! A spindle!"

"Huh?" Lottie mutters.

I am thinking the same thing.

Sleeping Beauty ignores Lottie. She rushes right to the sewing contraption and stops short an inch away.

"Future life, future prince, here I come," she says dreamily, reaching her hand out toward the spindle.

What does she mean? She *wants* to touch the spindle on purpose? She *wants* to prick her finger?

"Ouch!" she cries as the needle pierces her skin. A speck of blood pops up on her finger.

Here we go! I stay in my hiding spot and wait for her to swoon into a deep sleep. Then we can get back to the task at hand: waking Robin.

I continue waiting.

And wait some more.

Sleeping Beauty just stands there.

She is not falling asleep. She is not even yawning.

Uh-oh.

I know what this means.

We messed up another fairy tale.

* chapter five *

Oops, We Did It Again

You're supposed to fall asleep!" Lottie shouts at the princess. She jumps off her bench and stomps her foot against the hard floor, looking very annoyed.

Jonah and I exchange a glance. I don't know what to do. Should I speak up or stay hidden behind the bed?

"I don't understand, either," Sleeping Beauty says, rubbing her forehead. "Since the day I turned fifteen I've been searching *everywhere* for a spindle. *Everywhere.* Behind chairs. In closets. Under stairs. Now I finally find one, I prick my finger on it, and

I don't fall asleep? How is that possible? I'm supposed to fall asleep for a hundred years and be woken up by my prince in the future!" She shoves her finger back at the spindle and pricks herself again. "Why. Isn't. This. Working?!"

I thought she was the clueless princess who wandered into the attic and touched the spindle by accident!

"Um. Hi," I finally say, rising from my hiding place. "Don't be alarmed. We're just two kids who happen to be in our pajamas. We're confused about what's happening here. You know about the curse?"

"Of course I know about the curse!" she hollers. She's clearly too upset to be curious about who we are. "My parents are obsessed with the curse! They've been warning me about spindles for years. Don't go near them; don't touch them; be careful, if you prick your finger you're going to fall asleep for a hundred years, blah, blah, blah. They won't stop talking about the dangers of spindles."

I shake my head in disbelief. "Then why did you touch one?"

The princess's face turns even pinker. "Because it's my destiny! Because living a hundred years from now will be amazing.

I bet in a hundred years you won't have to climb a thousand stairs to get to an attic. You'll just get inside a small box, press a button, and be pulled to the top!"

"You mean an elevator," Jonah says, standing up, too.

The princess frowns. "I don't know what that is. And I don't understand who you two are. Or you," she says, motioning with her pricked finger to Lottie. "But I do know that a prince is supposed to wake me. And that would just be the beginning. My life was going to be perfect." She closes her eyes and wears a pained expression.

"What could be wrong with your life now?" I wonder aloud. "You're a princess!"

"A *cursed* princess," Jonah adds.

"Still," I say. "There are way worse curses." Then I glance back at Sleeping Beauty. "But you are right. Your prince was going to wake you, and you were going to get married and live happily ever after."

She frowns at me. "How do you know?" she asks. "Are you from the future?"

"Kind of," I say. "Where I live, we know your whole story from beginning to end."

Lottie nervously bites her thumbnail. "I can't believe it didn't work," she mutters. "My mother is going to freak."

Huh? "Who's your mother?"

"Carlotta!" she replies. "The thirteenth fairy!"

Sleeping Beauty gasps. "The thirteenth fairy!"

What? "Lottie's mother is the thirteenth fairy?" I guess she isn't the villain herself, but daughter of a villain is close enough.

"Yes," Lottie says. "I'm Carlotta the Second. Lottie."

"But you're so old! How old is your mother?" Jonah asks. "A hundred?"

"No," Lottie titters, and nibbles her pinkie nail. "She's seventy. Since her retirement, I've taken over her wand and all her fairy responsibilities. Including you." She nods toward Sleeping Beauty. "This is terrible. Absolutely awful. I have to tell my mother what happened at once. She's going to be very upset." With a poof of sparkle, Lottie disappears.

"Wait!" Sleeping Beauty calls out, but it's too late. "Now what? Why didn't the spell work?"

I look at Robin and then back at Sleeping Beauty. Robin is asleep. Sleeping Beauty is awake. I clear my throat.

"I'm sorry, but I think my friend Robin accidentally used up your spell."

"Who?" Sleeping Beauty asks, but then she notices Robin lying on the bed with her eyes shut. "Is that Robin? Why is she sleeping? Who is she? And who are you people? Can someone explain what's happening?"

"I'm Abby," I say, standing up straight. "And this is my little brother, Jonah. It's a pleasure to meet you."

"Hey, there," Jonah says. "Is your real name Sleeping Beauty?"

"No," she says. She sits down on the bench and slumps. "It's Princess Brianna."

Jonah nods. "Can I call you Bri?"

"Sure," Brianna says. "I like it. It sounds almost . . ."

"Like a cheese," I say. A delicious, fancy cheese — but still a cheese.

"Like a name from the future," she finishes, brightening. "Brianna is such an old-fashioned name. And I am all about the future."

"Maybe you should try the spindle thing again," Jonah says.

Princess Brianna pokes her pinkie against the needle and winces. "This finger is a lot more sensitive than the other one. And it still didn't work!" She glares at Robin. "Did that girl really use up my spell?"

"Seems that way," I say sheepishly.

Her shoulders sag. "Does that mean she's going to marry my prince, too?"

"Oh, um, no," I say. "No way. She can't stay asleep for a hundred years. She needs to wake up. Soon. We need to get home. Her mother is picking her up at ten."

I glance down at my watch. Then I realize I am not wearing it. Argh. I took it off before bed. I was not expecting to go kingdom-hopping tonight.

"Never mind. What time is it *here*?" I ask.

"It's just after lunch," Bri says. "Around twelve forty-five."

Time back home is always slower than time in fairy tale kingdoms. When we were in the kingdom of Mustard, every hour at home was a day in fairy tale land.

Hmm. Maybe a hundred years here isn't long at all. Maybe a year here is only a day at home. Or maybe a year here is only a minute at home. So a hundred years will pass in a hundred minutes. That's less than two hours.

"If only we knew what time it is back home," I sigh. I gaze out the skylight and into the clouds. It's getting gray out there.

"It's a quarter to one back home," Jonah says.

I look down at him. "How do you know that?"

He waves his electronic game in front of me. "This tells the time."

"Wait. You've had that with you all along?"

He nods. "It was in my pajama pants between my tummy and the elastic band."

I grab the game and see that it does indeed tell the time. Twelve forty-seven, to be exact. "You're lucky you didn't lose it."

He snorts. "You're lucky I know what time it is."

I shove the game back at him. "If it's twelve forty-seven during the day here and twelve forty-seven in the middle of the night *there*, then, even though there is a twelve-hour time difference, time is passing at the same speed here as it is back home."

"So a hundred years here is a hundred years there," Jonah says.

My stomach sinks. "What are we going to do?" I turn to Robin and shake her by the arm. "WAKE UP, ROBIN, WAKE UP!"

Instead of waking up, she lets out a tiny snore.

What now?

⁂ chapter six ⁂

We Need a Plan

It's raining. HARD.

The water is loudly *click-click-click*ing against the skylight, and it's hard for me to think with so much noise.

Bri hasn't moved from the bench. She's spinning the wheel with her foot. "I can't believe this happened."

"I can't believe this happened *again*," I mutter. "But here's what I don't understand: If Robin activated the spell, shouldn't all of us in the palace have fallen asleep? That's what was supposed to happen."

"It was?" Bri asks. She stops spinning. "My family, too?"

I nod.

"Oh, that would have been so great," she says sadly. "They would have been with me when I woke up."

Jonah bounces on his exposed toes. "Imagine Lottie had put us all to sleep for a hundred years. Mom and Dad would have freaked out!"

I turn to Bri. "Doesn't the idea of sleeping for a hundred years scare you?"

Bri looks up at the skylight wistfully. "No. I've been waiting for this day since I was born. This" — she motions around her — "is me biding my time. I'm waiting for my real life to start. And now, because your friend stole my curse, it never will." She sighs. "I'll never get to see all the things that haven't been invented yet. Like ways to get around without horses. Or a boat that flies. Or faster ways to send messages to your friends."

"Cars, planes, and e-mail," Jonah says, and squats down on the ground.

"I don't know what those first two are," Bri says. "But

we do have mail without the E. My friend Tom's father is the mailman. He delivers messages across the land."

"Cell phones get messages to friends, too," I say.

Bri frowns. "What's a cell phone?"

"Something I don't have," I say with regret. "So I guess that means this place has no modern stuff?"

"If by modern you mean cars, planes, elevators, and cell phones, then no," Bri says. "Where are you from exactly?" Her eyes widen. "It really does sound like the future."

"Kind of," I say. "But not exactly."

"If I can't get to my future, maybe I'll go back with you," she says eagerly. "Do you have any princes where you live?"

"Not in Smithville," I tell her.

"Never mind, then," she says, spinning the wheel again.

The rain bangs harder against the skylight.

"Speaking of Smithville," I say, "we need to find a mirror or some sort of magical object that will take us back."

Bri pokes her thumb against the needle. "I'd suggest the spindle, but its magic appears to have been used up."

"True," I say. "We only have just over nine hours to figure it out, too. Robin's being picked up at ten."

"At least it's the weekend," Jonah says. "Otherwise Mom and Dad would wake us up at seven."

"Yeah, but they'll probably start wondering where we are if they don't see or hear any of us by nine thirty." A drop of water lands on my head. I look up. Terrific. Now the ceiling is leaking.

"If we find a portal home, we could always carry Robin back asleep," Jonah says.

Another water drop lands on my head and I wipe it away with the arm of my pajama top. "And then what? Won't her parents freak out when they can't wake her up? They'll think she's in a coma. No, we have to figure out how to wake up Robin here. Plus, find a magic portal. Plus, put Bri to sleep." I'm feeling overwhelmed. Another drop lands on my head, so I stand up. The bed creaks. "Let's start with waking Robin up and putting Bri to sleep."

"But how are we going to do that?" Bri asks.

"I don't know. What puts people to sleep?"

"Car rides," Jonah says. "I always fall asleep in the car."

"You drool, too."

"Do not!"

"Do so. Anyway, cars are not helpful."

"We should move Robin to the floor," Jonah says. "So Bri can lie down. Anyway, Robin looks way too cozy."

He has a point. Robin does look a little too cozy. Even on the burlap sack. "Jonah, you take her legs," I say. "Bri and I will take her shoulders. Ready? One. Two. Three!"

We pull Robin onto the floor. I feel bad, but it's for her own good. Kind of like a flu shot.

"Now you lie down on the bed," I order Bri.

She kicks off her red heels and does as she's told.

"Now we're in the right positions," I say. "I'll help Bri fall asleep, and Jonah, you help Robin wake up. 'Kay?"

Jonah's eyes light up. "I have an idea," he says. "Be right back."

"Be careful!" I tell him as he disappears out the door. I turn my attention back to Bri. "Do you want to take your crown off first? It doesn't look that comfortable."

"It's not, but I want the prince to realize I'm a princess, you know?" she says.

"Good point," I agree. I sit down at the edge of the bed beside her.

Bri adjusts her head on the pillow and closes her eyes. "What are you going to do?" she asks.

"Sing you a lullaby," I say.

She adjusts her position again. "I can't get comfortable."

"You need to relax."

She tosses and turns and turns and tosses. She loosens her gold sash. "Ready," she says finally. But then she squirms again. "Really ready."

I clear my throat. *"Rock-a-bye baby, on the tree top. When the wind blows, the cradle will rock. When the bow breaks the cradle will fall. And down will come baby, cradle and —"*

Bri's eyes jerk open. "How is this supposed to relax me? You're singing about a baby falling from a tree! The baby is going to break her poor little neck!"

"That's the way the song goes," I say. Hmm. She has a point. What if I change the words? "Let me try again. Close your eyes. Ahem. *Rock-a-bye Brianna, on the tower top. When the wind blows the . . . princess will rock. When the bed breaks, the mattress will fall. And down will come princess . . ."* My voice trails off.

"That is not much better."

"Sorry," I mumble.

Bri sighs. "Why don't you just hum softly?"

I nod. Then I hum. Robin closes her eyes.

I keep humming. *Hummmmmmmm*. Another drop of water lands on my head. Then on Bri's cheek.

"This isn't working," Bri says.

"Do you want me to find you some warm milk? That helps me fall asleep sometimes. Or maybe an eye mask? It's too bright in here because of the skylights, even with the rain. Where are we anyway? We're in a tower, right?"

"We're in the west tower," Brianna says. "At court."

"We're at a court?" I ask. My heart thumps. "Like criminal court?" I would love to see a court. Judges work in courts!

Bri shakes her head. "No. The royal court."

Oh. Right. Royal court. Oops. "So we're not in a castle?"

"No," she says. "But we're only a few minutes away." She closes her eyes again. "Maybe we should try counting turtles."

Did she say turtles? "You mean sheep, right?"

She shakes her head. "No, I mean turtles. Why would you count sheep?"

"Um . . . I don't know. Because they're kind of fluffy? They look like clouds. Why turtles?"

"Because they're slow walkers."

Can't hurt. "One turtle. Two turtles. Three turtles —" I feel ridiculous counting turtles but at least Bri looks more relaxed, so I keep going.

I try to imagine them. Little turtles. Green turtles. Slow turtles.

"Four turtles. Five turtles. Six." Bri looks like she's relaxing even more. This is working! Her breathing just got heavier, too. I wave my hand over her eyes and she doesn't move. I think she's sleeping! I should keep going, though, so her sleep gets really deep.

"Seven turtles. Eight turtles. Nine turtles." Yawn. Maybe I should lie down, too? My arms are feeling kind of heavy. "Ten turtles. Eleven turtles." I curl up at the bottom of the bed. "Eleven turtles." Did I already say eleven? I think I did. Oh well.

It can't hurt if I close my eyes for a few minutes, can it? I'm tired. It's the middle of my night, after all.

Eyes. Heavy.

So very heavy.

I'm so very ti . . .

✳ chapter seven ✳

Good Morning!

*B*ANG! BANG! BANG!

My eyes fly open. What is that? Where am I?

BANG! BANG! BANG!

I open my eyes. Jonah is smashing together two copper pots directly above me.

I realize I'm lying in a very uncomfortable position on the bed, my head at a ninety-degree angle. Bri is sleeping on the other end. Robin is sleeping on the floor beside me. Everything that's happened rushes back to me.

"What are you doing?" I whisper to Jonah while waving frantically. "Stop!"

"I'm trying to wake up Robin," Jonah says.

"I just put Bri to sleep," I whisper back.

But it's too late.

Bri is groaning in bed, her eyes open. She is covering her ears with her hands. "Has it been a hundred years? Are we in the future?"

"No," I say. I pry the pots out of my brother's hands. "My brother ruined our plan."

"But I was asleep," Bri complains. "I really was."

I glare at Jonah. "What were you thinking?"

He scowls. "She's supposed to sleep for a hundred years. Once we put her to sleep, I didn't think she was going to wake up. It was a curse."

"He has a point," I admit, staring at my sleeping friend. "I don't think any amount of noise will wake up Robin."

"So what *will*?" Jonah asks.

That's when it hits me. "A prince! A prince will wake her up! That's what the twelfth fairy said and that's what happens in the story. A prince kisses her and that's when she wakes up. We need to find a prince."

"Great idea," Jonah says. "Do you know any princes?"

"Do I? No. But Bri must know a couple." I glance back at Bri. "Don't you have prince-and-princess mixer dances or something?"

She shakes her head. "I have friends who are dukes and duchesses. My parents think I'm going to marry one of the dukes, but I'm so not. Oh, and I have one friend who's a commoner. Tom. We've been friends since we were babies. He's really great. Very smart. And sweet. And funny."

"But he's not a prince?" I ask.

"No."

I sigh. "Then he can't help us."

Bri rubs her forehead with the palm of her hand. "Are we sure wearing a sleep mask won't help me? Or maybe throwing cold water on your friend will do the trick?"

Jonah licks his lips. "Speaking of water, I'm thirsty. Do you have any soda?"

"Jonah, can you please focus?!" I say. I turn to Bri. "I'm

sorry. Little brothers are so annoying. Plus, Jonah knows he's not allowed to have pop." Or soda as Jonah now calls it since we moved to Smithville. I'm sticking to calling it *pop*, thank you very much.

"Little brothers are annoying," Bri says. "Felix is such a thorn in my side."

"Who's Felix?" Jonah asks.

"My little brother," Bri says.

"I wish I had a little brother," Jonah says wistfully. "At least he wouldn't boss me around."

"I didn't know you had a little brother," I say to Bri. "I thought your parents had a hard time having kids."

"They did. He was a surprise baby. He's much younger than me — only three."

"Aw," I say. "That's so cute."

"Did he have a magical gift party when he was born, too?" Jonah asks.

"Are you kidding me?" Bri asks incredulously. "No way. My parents wouldn't let any fairies near him after what happened with me."

Just then a loud trumpet noise blares.

I check to see if it woke Robin up.

It didn't.

"That trumpet blast means my parents and brother are back at court," Bri says. "They'll be serving tea now if you're still thirsty, Jonah."

"He doesn't drink tea," I say. "But he can have some milk." I look up at the skylight. The sky still looks gray, but the *click-click-click* noises have stopped. "At least it's not raining anymore."

"For now," Bri says. "April is a rainy month in our kingdom. We should move while it's dry."

"It's April here? It's only November in Smithville!" I guess it's not only the time that's different here — the months are different, too. "What's the name of this kingdom?" I ask.

"Is it Ketchup?" Jonah pipes up hopefully.

Bri looks puzzled and shakes her head. "No. It's the Kingdom of Rose."

"Like the flower?" I ask.

She nods.

"Roses are my favorite flower," I tell her. I can draw them well. All you need to do is make small half circles going outward. They're one of my best doodles. Well, roses and judge gavels.

Oh, I wish this were a criminal court.

"Do you guys have a lot of roses?" Jonah asks.

Brianna nods. "They're everywhere."

"*That's* the sweet smell!" I exclaim. I take a big sniff. "It's delicious."

Bri shrugs. "I don't notice it anymore. I'm used to it. C'mon, let's go get Jonah something to drink at Rose Abbey. That's the name of the castle."

Rose Abbey? The castle has my name! Kind of! Cool!

"Before we go can we move Robin back to the bed?" I ask. "I don't want to just leave her on the floor."

The three of us heave Robin back to the bed. She keeps on sleeping, of course. Then Bri, Jonah, and I walk back down the stairs. Walking down is easier than walking up, but the view is scarier. Since the tower is all open space I can see how far the drop is to the bottom.

"Where were your parents?" I ask Bri as we make our way down.

"At a yard sale."

"Why would a royal family want to shop at a yard sale?" I ask, frowning. "Don't people sell used stuff?"

"Yes," Bri says. "My parents love used stuff. They're bargain hunters and they're shopaholics."

"Really?" I ask. That isn't exactly how I pictured a king and queen.

Bri nods. "My mom and dad are obsessed. Look down. Do you see all the stuff? Pots. Pans. Plates. Glasses. Sheets. Lamps. That's what all the piles down there are."

I'm too afraid to look down again, but I remember the piles from when we arrived.

"That's where I found the pots," Jonah says a few steps behind me.

"My parents use all the towers for storage," Bri says. "They're especially keen on kitchen stuff. Bowls, plates, and glasses. They're also obsessed with farmers' markets. They buy a ton of food. We have three pantries in the palace kitchen."

"Good," Jonah says. "Because I'm starving. Can I get a snack, too?"

"Absolutely," Bri says.

"Do you like cheese and crackers?" Jonah asks. "I bet you like Brie cheese. If there was a food called Jonah, I would eat it all the time."

If there was a food called Abby, I would want it to be something sweet. But not too sweet. It would have to have a little bite. Salted caramels, maybe? But I don't need a food named after me. I already have a castle!

"How come you didn't go to the yard sale with your family?" I ask.

Bri reaches the bottom and turns around to face us. "I wanted to try and find the spindle," Bri explains. "I knew there had to be at least one somewhere. . . . Anyway, I don't want someone else's old junk. What do I need that for? They'll have everything I need in the future."

"Your parents didn't mind that you stayed home?" I ask Bri, remembering from the fairy tale that Sleeping Beauty's parents were very protective.

Jonah and I finally reach the bottom. There really is a lot of stuff here.

Bri maneuvers her way through the piles. "I told them I wasn't feeling well and promised I would stay in bed. And that wouldn't have been a lie if my plan had worked out the way it was supposed to."

When we push open the door to outside, a cool breeze washes over me. Ah. It's nice out here. We step onto a path that cuts through a rose garden.

There are roses *everywhere*. Red roses, pink roses, white roses, apricot roses, purple roses, orange roses . . . there are even yellowy-green ones. The kingdom of Mustard would love those. The garden is divided into square patches, each about five feet by five feet, and each square has a different color rose.

I really wish I had shoes on. I do not want to step on a thorn.

"Too sweet, too sweet," Jonah whines, blocking his nose. "It's making me sick."

"Jonah!" I shoot him a warning look. "You're being rude!"

"I don't even smell them," Bri says.

I don't know how she doesn't smell them. The scent is pretty strong. "I've never seen so many roses."

"We've had them forever," Bri says. "The entire economy of the kingdom revolves around roses. We make rose teas, rose medicines, rose-petal jams . . ." Her voice trails off. "But if you're scared of bees, be careful because we have quite a few buzzing around."

"Who's *not* scared of bees?" I wonder out loud.

Bri shrugs. "I'm not. They're so small."

She's so brave. I wish someone had given *me* courage when I was born. Probably more useful then the giant brown bear my great-aunt sent me.

"Court is shaped like a diamond," Bri explains. "There's the west tower, north tower, east tower, and south tower. Around the towers is the rose garden and then a gate for security. In the center is Rose Abbey. Follow me."

We walk around to the other side of the tower and that's when I see the palace. It's about four floors high and very square looking. It's made of stone, and has large windows all over it. It looks like the outside of a ski chalet. Definitely less *castle-y* than the others I've seen.

"There's my family," Bri says, pointing to a black carriage outside the castle door. "I guess I'll tell them I'm feeling better."

A tall man in a long, red velvet robe steps out of the carriage. He's wearing a gold crown and holding a large silver wok in his arms.

"Look what we got!" he announces to the three royal servants awaiting his arrival.

"Good find, King Morris!" the servants say in unison.

"That's my dad," Bri says.

A woman steps out of the carriage next. She's also wearing a red velvet robe and a gold crown. She's holding a glass bowl.

"Good find, Queen Vickie!" chirp the servants.

"My mom," Bri says.

And finally a little boy wearing red pants and a black shirt jumps out of the carriage. He has a small gold crown on his head. He's holding a wooden spoon.

"Good find, Prince Felix!" the royal servants exclaim.

"Wait a sec," I say, stopping in my tracks. "Felix is a prince?"

Bri nods. "Of course he's a prince. He's my brother." She slaps her palm against her forehead. "He's a *prince*!"

"He's a prince!" I repeat.

"I don't get it," Jonah says. "We know he's a prince. So what?"

I turn to my brother. "All we need to do is get him to wake up Robin, and at least one of our problems is solved."

* chapter eight *

Oh, Brother

brianna!" the king calls. "You're up! Come see what we got!"

"Don't say anything to them about what happened, got it?" Brianna whispers to Jonah and me as we follow her to meet her parents.

"How come?" Jonah asks.

"Because they'll freak out. They're still really upset about the curse. That's why they're so obsessed with buying kitchen stuff. They're mad at themselves for not having enough plates and not inviting all the fairies. So just don't say anything. Promise?"

"Promise," we say as we approach the front door of the palace, where the king and queen are standing.

The queen and king give Bri a big hug. Up close I can see that Bri has her mom's blond hair and upturned nose, but she has her dad's dark-blue eyes and pink cheeks.

"We missed you at the yard sale!" the king says in a booming voice. "Are you feeling better?"

Bri nods. "Much. I invited some friends over to keep me company." She gestures to Jonah and me. "They're commoners."

Gee, thanks.

"Would they like to come inside for some tea?" the queen asks, motioning toward the door.

"Do you have any soda?" Jonah asks.

I elbow him in the side. "No soda. I mean, no pop!"

"Fine," he grumbles. "Milk?"

"Of course," the queen says, and enters the palace.

Inside, it's cool and still smells like roses. My nose is not getting used to the rose scent and I hope it never does.

The floors are covered in different rugs. Every inch of wall space is covered in paintings, large and small. Every surface is covered in vases filled with bouquets of different colored roses and bowls filled with rose potpourri. There are also large candles everywhere.

"Wow," Jonah says. "You guys have a lot of stuff."

"Yes we do!" the queen cheers. "Do you like the new rug we got last week?" She points to a white rug under a coffee table. "Isn't is grand?"

I'm not sure if *grand* is the word I'd use. More like *shaggy*. But I nod anyway.

I'm not sure how, but the room looks funky. It has style.

Seeing all this *stuff* reminds me that we have *three* tasks — not two — to get done. Yes, we have to wake up Robin and put Bri to sleep, but we also have to find the enchanted object that will take us home. Sometimes it's a mirror, but sometimes it's a chimney or a cauldron. This palace is crammed with stuff. The object could be anything.

Since it's probably already about two o'clock, and if we want to be home by nine thirty, before our parents start to wonder about us, we have only seven and a half hours to find it. Although usually the portal pops up when we're ready to go . . .

My heart rate speeds up. So much to do. So little time. Usually we're in these fairy tales for a few days, at least, and we have only two tasks. This time we have only a few hours and we have three tasks. We need to get this show on the road. We need to get Bri's brother to Robin in the tower.

Hmm. Where is Felix?

The king and queen lead us into the royal dining room. Royal servants come in carrying trays of pastries, a large pot of tea, and milk. The pastries are really pretty. One is a tower of fluff and almonds and raspberry drizzle. It will be hard not to get distracted.

We all sit down at the table.

I make sure to put my napkin on my lap and motion for Jonah to do the same.

My brother downs a cup of milk and then grabs a chocolate scone.

I take a pastry. Then another. Traveling to fairy tales makes me hungry.

"Are you two going to take a nap?" the queen asks me, sipping elegantly from her teacup.

"A nap? No, we're too old to nap," I say, but then I realize that she's looking at our outfits.

We're wearing our pajamas.

Why am I always wearing pajamas whenever I meet royalty? It's so embarrassing.

Having a pair of shoes on wouldn't be so terrible, either.

A large crash comes from another room.

"Felix!" the queen hollers. "What are you doing?"

"It wasn't me!" a squeaky voice yells back.

The king and queen both laugh.

Bri rolls her eyes. "It was so him."

Felix dashes through the room and smacks right into the table. "Not me again!" he cries. Up close he looks exactly like the king, but little. Same dark-blue eyes and spiky hair.

"Stay where we can see you," the king orders.

"Look at me!" Felix calls, and launches himself into a cart-wheel and then into a side table. A vase of roses plummets to the floor.

He straightens up, yells "Girls are gross!" and pinches his sister's arm.

"Ouch! Mom! Did you see that?" Bri calls out.

"See what?" the queen asks. "Isn't your brother adorable?"

Um . . . he does not seem so adorable. He seems more like a little monster. I almost expect to see skid marks on the floor.

He runs around the room a few more times before crawling into an empty chair.

We all munch silently. Mmm. Raspberry-almond-fluff pastries are *gooooood*. Next time I have a sleepover I'm making these instead of s'mores.

After a few minutes, the queen folds her napkin and places it on the table. "Bri, keep an eye on your brother."

Then the royal couple wave to us and head off to another room.

Felix pops out of his chair and marches over to Jonah. "Who are *you*?" he demands.

"I'm Jonah," my brother says, giving the little boy a smile.

Felix narrows his eyes. "I don't like to share. Are you going to take my toys?"

Jonah's smile falters. "No."

"Play with me!" Felix pokes Jonah in the side with his wooden spoon. "You have to play with me!"

Jonah scoots his chair sideways. "Stop it."

Bri crosses her arms. "Felix, we need your help with something in the west tower."

Felix grabs an unlit candle off the table and lies facedown on the ground. "No."

"Come on, Felix," Bri says with a sigh. "Please."

"No." He turns his head toward us and sticks out his tongue.

Now what? I can't believe I thought Jonah was annoying. Felix is a hundred times more annoying and I've known him for only five minutes.

"Pretty please with a cherry on top?" I ask, my voice sweeter than raspberry drizzle.

Felix flips onto his back and balances the candle on his little feet. "What will you give me?"

"Excuse me?" What nerve this little boy has! Then I add, "You may want to be careful with that candle." I can't help it. Once a big sister, always a big sister.

Felix ignores me and tries balancing the candle with only one foot. "You want me to come with you. Sounds like you need me. So what do I get?"

Bri stands up and grabs the candle off his foot. "What do you want?"

He points to Jonah. "I want him to give me a horseyback ride to the tower."

"You mean piggyback?" I ask. "When you carry someone on your back?"

Felix stomps his feet. "Horseyback! Horseyback!"

"Same thing," Bri says with a nod.

"Fine," Jonah says with a shrug. He stands up. "Horseyback does make more sense if you think about it."

Felix jumps up and onto Jonah's back in about three seconds flat. Then he hits my brother on the head with his spoon. "Go, horsey, go!"

Jonah frowns but obeys.

Giddyup.

* chapter nine *

Kiss, Kiss

Felix insists that if we want him to go upstairs, Jonah will have to horseyback him *all* the way there.

There are about eighty stairs.

By the time we're halfway up, my brother's face is the color of a tomato. No — of a red rose.

"So now you know what it's like to have a little brother," I tell Jonah with a laugh.

He grunts in reply.

"Faster, horsey, faster!" Felix commands.

I have met a lot of princes through the magic mirror, but he is the most demanding BY FAR.

Once we're finally at the top, Felix hops off and Jonah slumps against the wall.

"This better work," Jonah mumbles.

Felix launches himself into another cartwheel. "There's a girl sleeping on the bed!" he cries.

"Yes. We need you to help our friend Robin wake up," I say.

His face scrunches up in horror. "Nooooooo!" he shrieks. "No way! I'm not helping a girl!"

"You said you would help us," Bri says. "That was the deal. Jonah gave you a horseyback and now you have to help us."

Jonah, meanwhile, has spread out on the stone floor. He is panting.

"No," Felix says. "I said I would come with you if he gave me a horseyback. I did not say I would help a girl."

"Jonah will horseyback you around the room again if you help," I pipe up.

Jonah groans. "I will?"

"No," Felix says. "I want his box."

"His what?" I ask.

"His box! The box that fell out of his pajamas when he was horseybacking me up the stairs. I want it."

"No way," Jonah snaps. "He can't have my game."

"Yes way," Felix says. "Or forget about me helping you!"

"But we need it to tell the time," Jonah says. "Right, Abby?"

"Not technically," I say. "Since we know that time here is the same as time at home. And I spotted a clock on top of a pile of plates downstairs."

Jonah gives me the stink eye.

"Give it to me," Felix orders.

Jonah reluctantly hands over the game, grumbling to himself.

Felix runs up to Robin and stops short in front of her ear.

"WAKE UP!" he screeches. "WAKE UP!"

She doesn't move.

"Can I pinch her?" he asks.

"Um . . . gently," I say.

He pinches her, not so gently, on the arm.

She still doesn't budge.

"She's not waking up," he tells us. "Should I poke her with my spoon?"

In the story, it's the prince's kiss that finally wakes up Sleeping Beauty. "Can you try, um, giving her a quick kiss on the cheek?" I suggest.

I brace myself for a shriek. I expect him to fall back on the floor and throw a tantrum. I expect him to ask for a million dollars.

Instead, he leans over and kisses Robin's cheek with an ear-shattering *smack*.

Bri shrugs. "He likes giving kisses."

We wait for Robin to open her eyes.

She doesn't.

"Robin?" I ask. "Are you awake?"

No answer.

Argh! "It didn't work," I say. "Why didn't it work? A prince tried to wake her up! He even kissed her! That's what happened in the original story! A prince kisses Sleeping Beauty and she wakes up!" I turn to Bri. "What did the twelfth fairy say, exactly?"

"That I would be woken up in a hundred years by a prince," she says.

"Then maybe a prince can wake her up only *after* a hundred years," Jonah says, still on the floor. "Not today."

That is a big problem. Huge. Ginormous! Wc can't wait for a hundred years to pass! How are we ever going to wake her up?

"There's only one thing that's going to fix our problems," I say.

"What's that?" Bri asks.

I sigh. "Magic. We should talk to a fairy."

"I don't know any fairies," Bri says. "Except Lottie. But she disappeared."

"Sometimes knocking on stuff works," Jonah says. He knocks on the wall. "Hello? Lottie? Are you there? Are any other fairies there?"

No one answers.

"We can't knock on *everything* in the royal court, " I say. "The king and queen have a lot of stuff."

"Can't we ask the king and queen to call a fairy?" Jonah asks. "They invited twelve over when you were born," he reminds Bri. "They probably know where to find one."

Bri shakes her head. "No way. My parents will never let me invite a fairy over. They've hated fairies ever since that day."

"I hate fairies, too!" Felix yells for no reason. Then he starts running in a circle around the attic. Again and again.

"Should I stop him?" I ask Bri.

Bri shakes her head. "He'll tire himself out eventually. Just leave him."

She's so patient! I wouldn't be that patient. Suddenly, I feel lucky to have Jonah. As far as younger brothers go, he's not so bad.

"So which fairy would we want to talk to?" I ask. "The twelfth one? She's the one who tried to help you in the first place. And it's her spell that made Robin fall asleep."

"Her name is Shaznay," Bri says. Then she bites her lip. "You know, I bet my friend Tom would know how to find her. His dad is the mailman. Tom used to help him with the deliveries."

"Let's call him!" I say.

"You mean yell his name out the window?" Bri asks, looking confused. "He lives outside the palace. He won't hear us."

"No, I meant using a phone. Which you don't have."

"Not yet," she says. "Though I bet I will in a hundred years."

"So how do we ask him?" I wonder. "No e-mail, no phones. What do we do?" I begin to panic. How will we talk to Tom?

Bri motions for us to follow her down the stairs. "We go to his house."

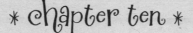

⚹ chapter ten ⚹

Everyone Wants a Tree House

We're about to walk over to Tom's — it turns out he lives just down the street from the royal court. But then a boy appears at the palace gate.

"Tom! Hi!" Bri says, smiling. "Just the person I wanted to see!"

Tom is about her age, fifteen, and very cute. He has wavy light-brown hair and freckles on his nose.

"You're just the person I wanted to see, too," he says with a laugh. "Which is why I came to visit."

"Hi, Tom!" Felix calls out, bounding over to him. "I have

a new friend named Jonah! His horseybacks are better than yours!"

"Better than mine? No way!" Tom exclaims, pretending to be shocked. "He'll have to give me a horseyback lesson."

Jonah puffs up with pride.

"Tom, meet my friends Abby and Jonah," Bri says. "They're commoners, too!"

Tom grins. "Nice to meet you, fellow commoners. We should get matching commoner shirts made."

Jonah and I laugh. I like Tom. He *is* funny.

"I have great news," Bri announces, her eyes sparkling. "I found the spindle!"

Tom's face falls. "Where?"

"In the west tower! Can you believe it?"

"But . . . what happened? How come you're not asleep? Wait, I know! Did you have too many cups of tea this morning?"

She laughs. "Of course not. The whole thing is complicated, but basically another girl touched it first and now she's asleep instead of me."

"That is *great* news," Tom exclaims. "So you're not going to sleep?" he says hopefully.

"No, I am," Bri says. "Or I will be. We just have to get a fairy to fix the spell."

His face falls again. "So you still want to sleep for a hundred years?"

"Of course I do," she says with a wave of her hand. "I'm not giving up that easily! It's my destiny. If I don't sleep for a hundred years, I'll never meet my prince."

Tom kicks a stone with the toe of his shoe. "Of course, of course, you've got to meet your prince. The hero who saves you from the curse. The best prince ever," he grumbles.

"Exactly," Bri says, failing to notice that Tom doesn't sound excited. "That's why we were on our way to your house. Do you know where Shaznay the fairy lives?"

He hesitates. "Yeah," he says eventually.

Bri smiles. I'm shocked to realize that it's the first time I've seen her smile since I've met her. Why doesn't she smile more? Is she *that* unhappy? She has a nice smile — I didn't realize she has a dimple on her left cheek. "Can you show us the way?" she asks.

"I guess I can," he says, sounding pretty unhappy himself. I get it — if Robin or Frankie *wanted* to sleep for a hundred years my feelings would be hurt, too. Best friends are supposed to want to spend time with you — not never see you again. "It's far, though," Tom adds. "We're going to need horses."

"Let's go to the stable," Bri says. She motions to me, Jonah, and Tom. But then she blocks Felix with her arm. "You're not coming with us."

Felix juts out his chin. "Yes I am. If you don't let me, I'm telling Mom and Dad that you're trying to find Shaznay."

She sighs. "Fine. You're so annoying. Come on."

The stable is between the south and west towers.

Bri gestures toward the stalls. "Pick whichever you want."

There are about twenty horses, all neighing, all smelly.

"Um, Bri?" I ask. "Aren't we all getting on one horse?" That's what we did when we were in the story of Snow White. We all climbed on one gigantic horse that took us around.

Bri saddles one of the horses. "Why would we do that? No. We'll each take our own. You know how to ride, don't you?"

"Yes," Jonah declares.

"You do not," I snap. "We don't."

"I'm sure it's not that hard," Jonah says, jumping on his toes. And I mean toes literally, since he still has no shoes on, only socks with holes in them.

"It's easy," Bri says. "You don't have horses in Smithville? How do you get places?"

"Our parents drive us in cars, which are carriages with no horses. Or if we're on our own, we take our bikes," Jonah says.

She leans in eagerly. "What's a bike?"

"It's a seat on two wheels. You pedal to make it move."

"That is *so* cool," Bri says. "I wish I had a bike. I bet there'll be bikes when I wake up from my hundred-year sleep."

I notice that Tom frowns when she says this.

"Could be," I say. "But what are we going to do right now?"

"You're going to get on Petals," Bri says. "That's Petals, not Pedals. Although maybe we should change it to make life more exciting around here."

I don't know. In my opinion, life is pretty exciting around here as it is.

Bri places a stool on the ground next to a horse. She motions for me to step up on the stool and helps me up onto Petals/Pedals's saddled back. "If Felix can do it, so can you."

Felix is already on a horse, wooden spoon in hand.

"There's a good boy," Bri purrs to Petals/Pedals.

My breath catches in my throat as I try to steady myself.

DO NOT BE AFRAID! ALSO, DO NOT FALL OFF!

Petals/Pedals doesn't look so scary. He's kind of cute. His mane is chocolate-brown and silky-looking. I just wish he were closer to the ground.

I carefully — oh so carefully — reach out to pet him. Awwww. He's soft!

"Hello, sweetie," I say. "You're not so scary, are you?"

"NEIGH!" he roars.

I close my eyes and scream.

"You'll be fine," Bri assures me. "I'm right beside you."

I slowly unclench my eyes. Everyone else is already on horses, staring at me. "Ready," I say, pasting on a grin. I am holding on to the reins so tight my knuckles have turned white.

"Off we go!" Tom calls back. He leads the way.

We trot through the opening of the gate and onto a dirt road. We pass other, smaller houses as we ride. Most of them have rose gardens, too, but none are as colorful or as plentiful as the gardens at court.

The clouds are gray but at least it doesn't rain.

A bee buzzes by my head. I'm not sure which animal I'm more afraid of — the bee or the horse. One is huge, one is tiny. Both are scary.

Thirty minutes later, Tom motions for us to pull up outside a group of massive trees. "We're here," he says, jumping off his horse.

Thank goodness. I look around. I don't see a house.

Jonah squints. "Is it an invisible house?"

"I bet they'll have invisible houses in the future," Bri says wistfully.

"Look up." Tom gestures toward the foliage.

Nestled above us in the tree branches is a house. A tree house.

"Oh, wow," Jonah says.

I have to agree. It is the coolest looking tree house I've ever seen.

The walls, floors, and roof of the tree house are made of glass.

Yes. Glass!

We can see right inside the house. I make out two purple chairs, a metal table, and even what looks like a yellow bean-bag chair.

"I want to live there!" Jonah says dreamily.

Bri jumps off her horse. "How do we get up?"

Tom points to a rope ladder that's dangling from the door. "We climb."

"Awesome!" squeals Jonah.

"Jonah! Horseyback!" Felix calls.

Jonah crouches. "Okay. Get on."

Is my brother crazy? I think he is. "Jonah, you cannot horseyback someone up a rope ladder! That's just not safe."

He waves my worry away. "You heard the kid. I'm really good at horseybacking. And it's not that hard. I climb things all the time."

He does go rock climbing with Mom on the weekends. But he doesn't rock climb while a three-year-old boy holds on to his neck and hits him with a wooden spoon.

"Not happening," I say. "I'm the older sister and I'm the boss."

"You are not."

"Am so!"

"Horseyback! Horseyback!" chants Felix.

"I'll stay with Felix," Tom offers.

"You sure?" I peer up at the rope ladder. It shudders in the breeze. "Because I really don't mind skipping this one."

"GIRLS ARE GROSS," yells Felix.

Never mind, then. I guess Tom stays and I climb.

"Follow me!" Jonah calls, and hurls himself toward the swaying rope ladder. Before I can even say, "Be careful," he's at the top, standing on a ledge.

A teeny, tiny ledge.

I wish he had on a helmet. I wish *I* had on a helmet.

I wish I had on a parachute.

Bri climbs up the rope and onto the ledge next, and then it's my turn.

* chapter eleven *

We Can See You

It takes me about five times as long as the others, but eventually I climb to the teeny, tiny top. When all three of us are steady, Bri rings the doorbell.

Since the door is all glass, we know someone's there. We see a woman sitting at her kitchen table sipping a cup of tea. I guess it's the fairy Shaznay. She's about my mom's age, maybe a little younger, and she's wearing a strapless white dress. She has light-brown skin and her brown hair is pulled back in a tight French braid.

She glances up and sees us looking at her.

A clear disadvantage to having a glass house is that you can't pretend you're not home.

Luckily, Shaznay seems happy to see us and hurries over to open the door. "Princess Brianna," she says warmly. "I haven't seen you since you were a baby. Come in, come in. Would you like some tea?"

People in the Kingdom of Rose really really like tea.

I step onto the glass floor and instantly wish I was back on the rope ladder. It feels like I'm stepping on ice that could break at any moment. *Do not look down*, I tell myself. *Do. Not. Look. Down.*

"No thank you," Bri says. "These are my commoner friends Abby and Jonah," she adds. I resist the urge to roll my eyes. "We're here to ask for your help. Remember the spell you did back when I was a baby? To make me not die?"

"Of course I do," Shaznay says, sitting back down.

"It got messed up," I say. Then I grip the side of the kitchen table in case the floor cracks.

Which doesn't make sense if you think about it. If the floor cracks, the table is going down, too.

That should give us a few hours to prepare. "We'll see you then," I say.

"Great," Shaznay says. "Which other fairies are you inviting?"

"Um, you're our favorite, so we're inviting only you," Bri says.

Shaznay smiles again. "That's very sweet, but if you want three *wifticals* you'll have to invite more than just me. I only grant one *wiftical* per birthday person."

"Can't you make an exception?" I ask.

She shakes her head sadly. "If I made an exception for you, I'd have to make an exception for everyone, now wouldn't I?"

"I thought she was the nice one," Jonah whispers.

"I guess we'll just have to invite more fairies to the party," I say.

Shaznay's eyes light up. "Fantastic! I haven't seen the other fairies in a while. No one's had a *wiftical* party since what happened at Princess Brianna's." She leans in closer to us and lowers her voice. "Are you going to invite Carlotta this time?"

I freeze. Isn't Carlotta the mother of Lottie? Wasn't she the one who cast the spell that almost *killed* Bri?

"No way," Bri says. "She's evil."

"We don't have to invite her. She retired," I say, feeling

relieved. "But we should probably invite her daughter. We don't want to upset anyone."

"I don't know," Bri counters. "She wasn't that helpful earlier today."

"We can't *not* invite her," I say. "Remember what happens when you don't invite everyone?" I mime pricking my finger and then a swoon. "I say we invite all thirteen fairies."

"At least they have enough plates this time," Jonah says.

"They have enough plates for the entire kingdom," I snort. "Hey, Shaznay, I have a question. Do you have to grant us the *wifticals* we ask for?"

She takes a long sip of tea. "We don't *have* to do anything."

"So we could get thirteen *wifticals* that we don't even want?" I ask. That won't solve any of our problems.

"I'd suggest that Jonah register for a *wigistry*," Shaznay says.

"A what?" I ask.

"A magical wish registry," she clarifies.

"What's a registry?" Jonah asks.

I turn to him to explain. "Remember when Auntie Jen got married and we went on her online registry and bought her an ice-cream maker? She had picked out a bunch of stuff that she wanted. It's like a wish list."

"Exactly," Shaznay says. "Just write out a *wigistry* on a piece of paper and leave it by the food at the party. The fairies will take a look and decide what they want to give you."

"I wish I'd been able to register," Bri says wistfully.

"Your parents registered on your behalf," Shaznay says. "And you got everything on the list. You are definitely the princess who has it all. Well, except what I was going to give you before I had to change mine."

"What were you going to give me?" Bri asks.

Shaznay smiles sadly. "Happiness."

Bri blinks. And then blinks again.

I can't help but feel bad for Bri. She has everything any girl would want — brains, courage, beauty, even the ability to play the piano — but she's miserable. Maybe she'll be happy in the future?

"Let's go," I say finally. "We've got a party to prepare for."

Bri, Jonah, and I wave good-bye to Shaznay and then we climb back down the rope ladder, this time all together.

I poke my brother with my foot. "You're turning ten, Jonah? Really?"

"Why not?" Jonah says, shimmying down. "I could be ten. Look what I can do!" He holds on to the rope with one hand and swings.

"Stop it, Jonah! Can you at least try to act like you're ten?" I'm holding on for dear life.

Bri reaches the ground first. "I don't know how we're going to throw a party. My parents won't allow it."

"Why not?" Jonah asks. "It's my tenth birthday!"

"Is not," I mutter.

"You're the one who said it was!" Jonah retorts.

"Maybe we can get your parents to leave *court*," I say. I emphasize the word *court* because . . . well, because I love it. *We're going to court! Take me to court! I'm going to be late for court!* If only I had a long black robe and a gavel. Then I'd really get to call all the shots. The rope ladder sways and I snap back to reality. Now is not the time for judge fantasies.

"How do we do that?" Jonah asks, stepping on the ground.

I'm the only one still on the rope. Two more steps . . . almost there . . . why does this fairy tale involve so much climbing anyway? I'd expect that if we were in *Rapunzel*, but *Sleeping Beauty*? Shouldn't we be doing more resting and napping?

Anyway.

"We can send them to another yard sale," I suggest, as I reach the bottom of the ladder and finally feel the ground beneath my feet. And by feet I mean my very, very dirty socks. My heart rate returns to normal.

"What if there isn't another yard sale today?" Bri asks.

"We can make one up," Jonah says.

"Jonah, when did you get so sneaky?" I wonder. "You want to send Bri's parents on a wild-goose chase?"

My brother smirks. "Exactly."

Bri nods. "It would have to be somewhere far away. So they're not back too quickly."

"We better get a move on," Tom calls out. "It's going to start raining soon." He and Felix are already back on their horses waiting for us. Felix is actually sitting on his sideways, which can't be safe.

A drop of water lands on my head. Again.

Too bad Sleeping Beauty doesn't know Mary Poppins. I could use an umbrella.

✳ chapter twelve ✳

Party Prep

by four o'clock — four P.M. in the Kingdom of Rose, four A.M. in Smithville — our party prep is in full swing. We're all very busy. The fairies will be here in two hours.

Luckily, the rain never came so our clothes are still dry. Also luckily, we didn't have to buy any supplies. Thanks to the king and queen, the court is stocked with stuff. Decorations, paper supplies, food . . . everything we want — they have. The pantries are like a Costco.

Not having to shop has given us time to do other things. So far we've:

- Made the king and queen a flyer telling them about an EVERYTHING MUST GO yard sale on the other end of the kingdom and then slipped it under their bedroom door.
- Made thirteen birthday party invites for Jonah's, ahem, tenth birthday.
- Sent Tom to deliver the party invitations to all the fairies.
- Decided to have the party on the ground floor of the west tower where we came through the mirror. This way all the royal servants won't see what we're up to.
- Blown up fifty blue and green balloons.
- Located another fifty balloons after Felix popped the first fifty.
- Picked chairs, tables, tablecloths, napkins, plates, teacups, cutlery, and vases out of the piles around us.
- Moved the extra tables, chairs, vases, pots, and other STUFF into the north tower.
- Swept the floor.
- Plucked different colored roses from the garden and arranged them in vases around the room.
- Sneaked tea, milk, sugar, bread, tuna, mayo, cheese,

cucumbers (we're making tea sandwiches, of course), celery, carrots, dip, a chocolate cake, and some of those yummy raspberry pastries out of the kitchen and into the tower without being detected.

While Bri and I prepare everything and Tom delivers the invites, Felix does somersaults, Robin continues to sleep upstairs, and Jonah sits on a stair and works on his *wigistry*.

He twirls a pencil between his fingers. "I can't believe I get to ask for thirteen magical things! This is the best day ever!"

"Not so fast," I say, tying the balloon I've just blown up. "We need some of those *wifticals*. You have to wish for the three things we need. You get only nine extras."

"Still! Nine *wifticals* is more *wifticals* than I had this morning. Or ever."

Hmm. Maybe letting him make his own *wigistry* is risky. Maybe I should write his list for him. Just to make sure he doesn't wish for anything crazy. Like a crocodile that does karate. Maybe he should wish for a cell phone.

He scribbles away.

"What are you writing, exactly?" I peek over his shoulder.

Number 1: Wake up Robin.

Number 2: Put Bri to sleep for 100 years until she's woken up by a prince.

Number 3: Make a magical portal so we can go back to Smithville.

Number 4: Make a crocodile that does karate.

I knew it! I try to grab the paper from him. "Jonah, you can't have a crocodile that does karate. Where is it going to live?"

"With us!"

"You're going to bring a crocodile back to our house in Smithville? Will it sleep in the bathtub?"

"It wouldn't fit in the bathtub." He scratches his head with the pencil. "Maybe I'll also wish for a swimming pool."

"Jonah, please be realistic. Write down things that won't eat us."

"Like a marker that squirts ketchup?"

"Um . . . okay. That could work. I'm not sure why you would want that, though."

"Who wouldn't want that? Oh! What about a puppy?"

Oooooooh. I have always wanted a puppy. If I had a puppy

I'd let him — or her — snuggle on my pillow every night. But my parents have always said no whenever I've asked for a pet. Too much work involved, they claim.

"Mom and Dad would never let us keep a puppy," I argue.

"They would if the puppy was adorable," Jonah says. "And magical. What should he be able to do?"

"Go grocery shopping?" I suggest. That might win over my parents.

"Babysit younger brothers?" offers Bri, while tying a balloon.

"Fly!" says Felix. He's hopping from chair to chair around the room.

"Yes!" Jonah exclaims. "Fly!"

"It's a bird, it's a plane, it's Superpuppy," I say.

Jonah squeals with laughter. "Superpuppy! That's awesome! I could get him a little doggy outfit with an S on it." His jaw drops, and then he scribbles on his paper. "I'm going to wish that I can fly, too!"

"SuperJonah?" I ask.

"Exactly! SuperJonah." He steps upon his chair, throws his arms out, and jumps. He lands with a thud.

Could this actually happen? What am I going to do if Jonah starts flying around the house? He'll always be able to watch what he wants on TV — he'll get to the remote faster. I'm starting to feel a little jealous. I want to be able to fly, too.

"Also," Jonah says, "I want to be taller."

"How tall?" Felix asks.

"A giant!" He reconsiders. "Maybe not. I have to be able to live in my house. I just want to be taller than Abby."

I flick him on the shoulder. "First we're the same age and now you're taller? Why don't you just wish you were born first and be done with it?"

His eyes widen. "That's a great idea!"

"ABSOLUTELY NOT." That is where I draw the line. Sure it would be cool to have an older sibling. But that older sibling should NOT be Jonah.

"I want to be taller!" Felix cries, stomping on a chair. "I want a flying puppy! I want a crocodile that does karate! I want to be SuperFelix!"

"Tough luck," Jonah tells him. "It's not your party. You don't get any *wifticals*."

"No fair!" he whines. "I want a *wiftical*! If I can't have one, I'm telling Mom and Dad!"

"You sure you don't want to add 'get a little brother' to your *wigistry*?" I ask Jonah.

He shakes his head. "No way. Little brothers are so annoying."

I giggle and ruffle Jonah's hair. Hah. I rest my case.

"I WANT A *WIFTICAL*!" Felix repeats.

"Okay," Jonah says. "You can add one thing to my *wigistry*. But that's it."

Felix smiles. "I want you to stay here. You're fun."

Jonah coughs. "Except that."

"Then I want a crocodile that can do karate."

"Fine," Bri says. "We can keep him in the moat."

I watch Jonah write down, *A crocodile that does karate for Felix*. I can tell by the look in his eyes that he's jealous, but he doesn't change his *wigistry*.

The door opens and I hold my breath. What if it's the king or queen? Will they stop us?

But no.

It's Tom.

"All delivered," he says. He's smiling but his eyes look a little sad.

"Great," I say. "I think we're almost done here, too. I'm just going upstairs to check on Robin."

I walk all the way up the stairs and open the door.

That's when I notice the problem.

Robin is gone.

✳ chapter thirteen ✳

How to Lose a Friend

She's missing!" I scream as I bolt down the stairs. My heart is beating a million miles a minute. I should never have left her by herself! This is all my fault!

"But where could she have gone?" Tom asks.

"Maybe she woke up," Jonah says.

I take a deep breath. "We have to find her. Now."

Either Robin woke up while we were gone and freaked out or she sleepwalked right on out of here. Either way she could be anywhere. My heart continues to hammer.

"What if something bad happened to her?" I moan. "What if she's on the road and runs into a horse? Or what if she wandered into the moat and drowned? Someone come look with me!"

Bri rubs my arm, looking sympathetic. "We'll find her; I promise. And we call it a moat, but it's really just a shallow pond behind the east tower. The gate should keep her on palace grounds. We'll all go look," Bri says.

Phewf. Robin couldn't have gotten that far, then.

We split up: Tom and the boys will start at the stables, then check the north and south towers, while Brianna and I will check the moat, the east tower, and then the palace.

As soon as we step out the tower door, I breathe in the scent of the roses. "You really can't smell them?" I ask Bri.

She shakes her head. "Not at all."

"That's so sad," I say. "They're amazing. Can we check the moat first?"

"Of course," she says.

The moat really is less of a pond and more of a puddle. "I'm not sure a crocodile that does karate will fit in there," I tell her, careful not to sound judge-y.

Get it? *Judge*-y?

"You're probably right," Bri agrees. "I'll ask Jonah to change it to a mini-crocodile. Or a teacup crocodile."

"Let's check the east tower next," I say.

"Let's go up," Bri says. "Instead of an attic, this tower has a roof deck. Maybe we'll be able to see her in the garden."

I guess that meant another fifteen flights of stairs. Hurrah. Not. But when we eventually make it to the deck, the view takes my breath away. The rose gardens look like a multicolored quilt spread out around us. In the distance are snowcapped mountains.

"Do you ever come up here just to take it in?" I ask Bri.

"No," she says with a shrug. "But maybe I should. It's nice."

"Nice? This isn't just nice. This is gorgeous." Bri is so strange. It's like she's immune to happy-making things. I wish they sold postcards of the mountain view so I could show Mom and Dad. Although then I'd probably have to explain where I was.

"I guess you're right," she says. "I should come up here more often." She doesn't sound like she totally believes it, though.

"We should keep looking," I say.

Next, we search the palace. Even though we were just in the kitchen and the pantries getting supplies we check them again since Robin could be on the move. Then we check in the library among the stacks of books, and in the ballroom, which is also home to a harp and a drum set and other musical instruments. No Robin.

"Your palace is really cool," I say. I'm pretty well-traveled in magical lands. At this point, I've seen a lot of palaces. The kingdoms of Zamel, Floom, and Mustard all had palaces, but I like this one the best. Sure, there are books and vases and candles and pictures everywhere, but the clutter and mishmash make Rose Abbey feel unique and homey. Like the stuff is supposed to be there. Also, even though it's cluttered, the floors are still sparkling and the windows shine because they're so clean. And it smells SO good.

Bri shrugs again. "It's okay."

"It's not just okay!" I tell her. "You should appreciate what you have *now*. Who knows what it will look like after no one takes care of it for a hundred years? I'm guessing it won't be so nice then."

She looks confused. "Why would no one take care of it?"

"Didn't I tell you? As soon as you fall asleep everyone else in the palace falls asleep, too. Your parents. The cooks. The maids.

Everyone who works at court. The palace is pretty much deserted after that. It's in shambles by the time the prince gets here."

"Oh, right." She bites her lip. "I hope we can clean it up."

"Maybe. I don't remember what the story says happens to it."

"We should check the bedrooms," she says, and leads me up the stairs. She hesitates on a step. "Does Tom fall asleep, too?"

"The story doesn't mention him specifically. It just says your family and the people who work in the palace. It doesn't say anything about friends."

She frowns. "That's too bad."

"But maybe there's no reason to worry about the palace," I say. "The spell was activated when Robin pricked her elbow, right? And none of us fell asleep. So maybe it'll be just you."

Bri pales. "Then what happens to my family?"

Isn't it obvious? "They stay awake."

"They never see me again?"

"They see you. You'll be asleep. But you never see them again, I guess."

She sniffs. Her brow crinkles. "That's so sad."

It *is* so sad. My heart hurts at the thought of it. I can't imagine never seeing my family again. It's too awful.

Suddenly, I wonder if maybe going to sleep for a hundred years isn't the best plan for Bri.

Maybe it's a *good* thing that we messed up her story.

"You don't have to do it, Bri," I say. "You don't have to go to sleep. You can just stay awake. And live now."

She closes her eyes and takes a deep breath.

There's the sound of a clock striking the hour from somewhere downstairs, and she opens her eyes. "No. I'll miss my family and my friends, but the prince is my destiny. He's going to make me the happiest girl in the world. We're going to get married. You said so yourself. The future will make me happy." She points down the hallway. "Let's check my room."

She opens the door to the most perfect princess room I've ever seen. The walls are a pale yellow, and the carpet is white and speckled with gold. To the right is what appears to be a massive walk-in closet. Directly ahead is a bay window. In front of the bay window is a canopy bed. A vase of yellow roses sits on a vanity table.

On the bed, fast asleep, is Robin.

Hurray! I run over to my sleeping friend and give her a hug. "I guess she *did* sleepwalk."

Bri's eyes widen in amazement. "She's even under the covers! She can do that in her sleep?"

I nod, feeling an odd sense of pride. "She walked down all the tower stairs, too, and those are seriously slippery. She's very talented."

Bri approaches us. "Shall we just leave her here until we get a fairy to reverse the spell?"

"I don't think so. I don't want her wandering off again. Do you have a wheelbarrow or something? But first . . ." I motion to my outfit. "Can I borrow a dress and some shoes to wear to the party? All I have with me are these pajamas and socks."

Bri leads me to her walk-in closet. "Of course. Take whatever you want."

There are at least a hundred dresses hanging there. Satin, lace, velvet, red, blue, black . . . sashes and frills and ruffles. Any kind of dress you want, it's here. They're organized by color. It looks like I'm standing inside a new box of colored pencils. "This is incredible," I breathe.

"What is?" Bri asks, searching through the outfits for something that might fit me.

"Your closet!"

"It's okay," she says with a shrug.

I can't take it anymore. "No! It's not okay! This is a dream closet. Don't you realize how lucky you are? I'm not saying that dresses are the most important thing in the world, but you have to at least admit that the things you have are pretty great! Wait a sec — is that an entire wall of tiaras?"

She nods. "Yeah. You can have one if you want. I barely even wear them."

"How could you not wear them? They're all so sparkly!"

She shrugs again. "I don't know."

"You're crazy, you know that?" I ask. She has all this amazing stuff, but she doesn't appreciate any of it.

"This should fit," Bri says, and hands me a knee-length blue dress with a corset top. I slip it on and tie it extra tight so it's not too baggy. The white sandals she lends me are too big but they'll do. Meanwhile, Bri puts on a beautiful pink ball gown and matching heels.

Suddenly, we hear voices outside the door.

"I think I'm just too tired to go out to another yard sale," the king says.

"Me too," says the queen. "Let's stay home tonight and relax."

Oh, no! "How are we supposed to have a party if they're home? The tower is only a few steps away from Rose Abbey," I say. "Do we have to cancel?"

"Too late now," Bri says. "It's almost six. We'll just have to keep the noise down and hope they don't pop by. Let's get moving." Bri picks up Robin, throws her over her shoulder, and hurries down the stairs.

"Wow. You're strong," I say.

"I know," she says. "Strength was one of my *wifticals*."

* chapter fourteen *

Party Time

bri, Jonah, Felix, Tom, and I are standing around the ground floor of the tower (now the party room). We're waiting.

Well, Felix is doing somersaults, but the rest of us are standing around.

The decorations are up. The food is out. Robin is back on her cot. We are ready.

I glance at the clock. "It's one minute to six! When do you think the fairies will start showing up?"

"Fairies are pretty punctual," Tom says. "They don't have a long commute."

At the same second the clock says six, sparkling puffs begin to pop up throughout the room. *Puff! Puff! Puff!*

Each one is incredibly loud. All together they sound like fireworks.

Thirteen women appear in the tower, including Shaznay and Lottie.

They don't look like fairies. They look like regular ladies. Mostly. They all have something slightly odd about them. One has bright-blue hair that's piled on top of her head. One is wearing platform heels. The platforms are a foot high — they look like stilts. One fairy is so small that she'd probably fit into my clothes, and I'm only ten.

Well, not *only* ten. Ten is pretty old. I glare at Jonah. It's a lot older than seven.

As soon as the sparkles disappear, all the fairies start squealing and hugging one another. Except for Lottie. She's standing by herself by the door, looking lonely and sad.

"Michelle! How are you?"

"I haven't seen you in ages!"

"You look smashing!"

"Claire, where have you been hiding?!"

Their voices fill the room. Jonah's fake tenth birthday party is clearly a fairy reunion.

"Where's the birthday boy?" the fairy called Michelle finally asks.

"Here I am!" Jonah calls out, waving his arms. "I'm turning ten!"

I roll my eyes at Jonah, but he avoids my glare.

The fairy in the high heels pinches his cheeks. "Happy birthday!"

"Happy tenth!" says the one with blue hair. Jonah grins, blushing a little. Oh, please. He's so loving the attention.

"Ten is the best!" chimes in Shaznay.

"And you must be his sister," says the teeny, tiny fairy.

I nod, brightening.

"How old are *you*?"

"I'm t-twelve," I lie. Well, why not? If he can claim to be ten, I can be twelve.

On the other side of the room, Bri is pouring the tea. Tom is walking around with a plate of sandwiches.

The fairies are flitting about, eating, drinking, and checking out the *wigistry*.

"Lottie doesn't look happy," Jonah whispers to me.

She's standing by the celery and she's definitely scowling. What's her problem? We invited her, didn't we? Her lips are pursed like she just sucked on a lemon, and her arms are crossed in front of her chest.

She's not hugging or saying hi to anyone.

Maybe she doesn't like tea sandwiches.

"Should we say something to her?" I wonder.

Jonah shakes his head. "No! What if she puts a mean spell on me?"

"She's going to cast a spell *for* you eventually. We may as well act nicely toward her now. Let's just go over and say hello. She doesn't seem to know anyone . . . maybe she'll be happy to have someone to talk to. I bet she's not really that bad." I march over to her.

"Hi, Lottie," I say.

"Hi," she says grumpily.

"So . . . have you seen Jonah's *wigistry*?" I ask.

"I have," she says tightly. "But I don't like to give people things off their *wigistry*. It's so *impersonal*."

"Oooookay," I say. "But that is why people create a *wigistry*, you know. So others don't have to guess what they like. This way, people can be given stuff they need."

"Oh, he needs what I'm giving him all right. Wait and see." Then Lottie cackles.

Uh-oh. I take a deep breath. *Don't be a curse, don't be a curse*, I mentally plead.

Just then, Felix runs across the room. Most of the fairies see him coming and move out of the way, but Lottie doesn't. Felix plows right into Lottie.

She yelps.

I hold my breath.

"It wasn't me!" he hollers.

With narrowed eyes, she trains her wand directly on Felix.

* chapter fifteen *

No Wrapping Paper Required

Who was it, then?" Lottie asks, her wand still pointing at Felix.

Felix looks back and forth between her and her wand. "All right," he admits, "It was me. Do you want to play Karate Crocs? It's fun." He waves it in front of her face.

Lottie hesitates. She slowly lowers her wand. She looks suspiciously at the game. She shrugs. "Okay."

Okay? Really?

Lottie offers Felix her hand and to my surprise Felix takes it.

The two go sit at a table. I can see them playing what used to be Jonah's game.

My brother pouts.

I'm just happy she didn't turn Felix *into* a croc.

"It's time for the *wifticals*," Bri calls out.

All the fairies gather around.

Jonah's pout turns into a smile. "I hope I get the things I asked for, really, I hope I do."

"I hope you do, too." I say. "Especially the ones we *need*."

The blue-haired fairy steps up. "Today, in honor of Jonah's tenth birthday —"

I roll my eyes.

"I bestow on him —"

Wake up Robin, wake up Robin!

"The power to fly!"

Seriously?

Jonah cheers. "I wanted that! I *really* did. Here comes SuperJonah!" My brother stretches his arms in the air. "Should I try right now?"

"No, Jonah. We're kind of busy."

"But I *really* want to try."

"Focus, Jonah!"

Another fairy steps up. "Today, in honor of Jonah's tenth birthday —"

Do they need to say that every time? It's enough already.

"—I bestow on him the ability to play the trumpet!"

Huh?

"That wasn't on my *wigistry*," Jonah whispers.

"They don't have to choose things from your *wigistry*," Bri reminds him. "A *wigistry* is just your suggested list. They can give you whatever they want."

"But we need them to choose the important stuff," I say, growing worried. "And he doesn't even have a trumpet."

"I can get one," Jonah muses. "I'll add it to the list."

I whack his shoulder. "Just stop."

Lottie leaves Felix to play Karate Crocs by himself and steps up next. My mouth goes dry. What's she going to do?

"On the occasion of Jonah's tenth birthday —"

I swallow. Hard.

"—I grant him a new pair of socks. His have holes in them."

Socks? Hurray! He can totally use new socks.

Jonah wiggles his toes. "I don't want new socks. Can *wifticals* be exchanged?"

"No. Just be glad it's not a curse," I hiss.

The teeny, tiny fairy steps up. "On the occasion of Jonah's tenth birthday —"

Blah, blah, blah.

"— I grant his request to allow Princess Brianna to sleep for a hundred years and to be woken up by a prince."

I perk up. One of our real requests! Bri is going to go to sleep! Hurray!

Everyone smiles. Even Bri.

Everyone except Tom.

His face tightens and he looks like he's blinking back tears. He looks like his heart is breaking in two.

Oh.

Oh!

His heart *is* breaking in two.

Tom loves Bri! He's not just her best friend. He LOVES her. It's so obvious now. And it's such a shame—he's such a sweet and funny guy. And he's going to lose her any minute.

"Should I lie down?" Bri asks, oblivious to Tom's feelings. "Is it going to happen right now?"

"Not this very second," the teeny, tiny fairy says. "All the *wifticals* go into effect as soon as Jonah blows out the candles on his cake."

We have the cake, but I don't think we took out birthday candles. "Bri, where are the birthday candles?" I ask.

She bites her lower lip. "We don't have any!"

I motion around me. "There must be some somewhere. Your parents have at least seven of everything."

She shakes her head. "They don't have *any* birthday candles. Trust me. We don't celebrate birthdays in our family, just in case. Birthdays remind my parents of *wifticals*. We have no birthday candles. They're terrified of them." She buries her head in Tom's arm. "What are we going to do? We don't have time to go buy them. We're doomed!"

Think fast, I tell myself. *Think fast!* "We'll just . . . make them." Yeah! We'll make them! How hard can that be?

Bri blinks. "We can't *make* birthday candles. At least, *I* can't make birthday candles."

"Of course you can," Tom says, turning toward her. "You can make anything you want. You're really creative. I remember the amazing towers you used to make with twigs and glue! You once built the entire royal court. It was really good," he says to me. "She made mini-roses and everything."

"I was six," Bri says. "I was just playing around."

I rub my hands together. "We can do this. All we need is wax and string." I grab my brother by his pajama top. "Jonah, run upstairs to the sewing contraption and get us some yarn for the wicks. Also, make sure Robin is still there."

He salutes us and takes off.

Bri stares out through the window. "Maybe we can take one of the bigger candles from Rose Abbey, melt it, and turn it into birthday candles."

"Great idea," I cheer. "We can do this!"

Hopefully. It actually sounds kind of complicated.

A minute later I hear Jonah call from a stair at the top of the tower, "Bri! Catch!"

She catches the ball of yarn between her hands and we run, run, run to Rose Abbey.

Once inside, we quietly search for a big candle. We do not want her parents to hear us.

"That mini–royal court replica I made took me months," Bri says. "Still, I can't believe Tom remembers it." She picks up one of four orange candles from the fireplace mantle. "How's this?"

"Of course Tom remembers it," I say carefully. "He's in love with you."

Surprised, she drops the candle onto the ground. "No he isn't!"

I bend to pick it up. "I'm pretty sure he is. Ninety-nine percent sure. Have you ever thought about marrying him instead of the prince?"

She shakes her head. "No — he's not the guy I'm supposed to marry. He's a commoner. He's just the buddy I hang out with while I wait for my prince to come."

"But, Bri, you don't even know the prince. Why would you choose him over Tom? I don't get it. Why would you rather live a hundred years from now when your life is so good right *now*?"

"I'm not happy," Bri says, grabbing a pair of scissors. "You heard Shaznay. The fairies didn't give me happiness. But I'll be happy in the future. When my real life starts."

I motion around me at the paintings and vases and carpets. "This is your real life!"

"No! It isn't. This is just . . . now."

I still don't get it. "Why are you so sure you'll be happy in the future?"

"Because! I'll have my prince. And there will be all kinds of cool stuff. Like . . . bikes! And phones!"

"Bikes, cell phones, and princes won't make you happy," I tell her. "You have to make yourself happy."

Her face is bright red. "That's what I'm *trying* to do," she insists. "I tried to prick my finger. Once I sleep for a hundred years I'll be happy!"

"But you don't need to wait a hundred years to be happy. Can't you see all the amazing things that you have right in front of you?" I reach over and pluck a pink rose from a copper vase. "Smell it! It's amazing!"

She shakes her head and pushes me away. "I don't want to talk about this anymore. Why don't you go back to the party and make sure our brothers aren't messing anything up? I can make the birthday candles myself."

She wants me to leave? "But Bri —"

"Just go," she snaps.

Tears prick my eyes. I didn't mean to upset her. But someone has to point out the truth to her if she's too blind to see it.

I arrive back at the tower just as Shaznay is granting her wish.

"This is the last one," Jonah tells me.

"On the occasion of Jonah's tenth birthday —"

Grumble.

"—I bestow a magical portal that will take him, his sister, and her friend back home to Smithville. This magic portal will be a window!"

Hurray! At least there are plenty of windows.

Although . . . maybe there are too many windows? How will we know which is the right one?

Jonah is jumping on his toes. "Abby, we did it! They gave us all the important ones. Even waking up Robin! And I'm getting a puppy with magical powers! Superpuppy! And an invisibility cloak, which I didn't even ask for but should have! Did you get candles?"

"Bri is making them," I say quietly.

He nods. "Did you write my name on the cake?"

"No."

"Shouldn't my cake say 'Happy Birthday, Jonah'?"

"What was I supposed to write your name with? Ketchup?"

He licks his lips. "That would be the best birthday cake ever. Abby! Look out the window!"

"Why? Which one? Is the portal home opening now?"

"No," he says. "But I think I just saw a person coming toward us!"

"Who? Where?"

I finally see where he's pointing. In the rose garden outside, someone *is* walking toward us.

It's the king.

✳ chapter sixteen ✳

Take One for the Team

O h, no! Is he going to stop us? I rush to the window and try to make out his expression. If he shuts down our party, we'll never get our *wifticals*.

"What's wrong?" Tom asks, sliding up beside me.

"The king is about to crash our party," I rush to explain. "We have to stop him! Or at least serve the cake first. Jonah, you stay here."

"I never get to do anything," he mutters.

"Oh, hush," I tell him. "Enjoy your tenth birthday party. You get only *two*."

Tom and I hurry out the door and close the door quickly behind us. Unfortunately we can still hear the party noises from outside.

"Hello, Your Majesty!" I call out.

"Hello there!" the king says. He doesn't look mad at all, which is good news. "I was wondering where you all were! Is Felix in there, too? Arc you guys having a party?"

"No!" I say just as Tom says, "Yes!"

Oops.

"Not a party party," Tom clarifies. "Just a small get-together."

He frowns. "Who's here?"

"Commoners," I say quickly. "Just a bunch of commoners. Kid commoners. No fairies," I add, but then cringe.

"How nice," the king says, and continues walking toward the door. "The queen and I are big fans of commoners. The queen is taking a rose-petal bath right now or I'm sure she'd want to come, too. Also, I need to fetch Felix. It's almost bedtime."

Just then, Bri steps off the path holding what looks like candles. When she sees her dad she stops in her tracks and shoves her hands behind her back. "Dad! Hi."

"I'll get Felix for you," I rush to say.

The king takes a step closer to the tower door. "Oh, that's all right. I want to come in and say hi."

"That's a great idea," Tom says.

It is?

"The commoners would love to see you. But before you go in, Brianna told me about the new rug you got at the yard sale last week," Tom continues. "I'm on my way home and I really want to see it before I go. And I heard you got some new paintings?"

The king smiles with delight. "Of course. Follow me. Tell the commoners I say hello," he instructs Bri kindly. "And tell Felix he can play a few more minutes, but then to return to Rose Abbey."

Tom leans over to us and whispers, "I'll distract him as long as I can. Good luck."

"Thank you," Bri whispers.

"Good-bye, Bri. I . . . love you." He blushes, turns away, and follows the king.

He loves her! I knew it!

Bri's jaw drops.

"See?" I say. "I told you!" Maybe she'll realize that Tom is the one for her. That choosing a prince she's never even met over her cute and sweet best friend is ridiculous. So what if he's a commoner? He's still her Prince Charming.

Jonah opens the door and peeks outside. "Guys? The fairies want me to blow out my candles. Do you have them?"

Bri stays frozen for a moment but then nods. "Yes," she says. She opens her palm and I see that she's holding eleven small orange birthday candles and a booklet of matches. The candles are lumpy and drippy but they're candles! "Let's do this. Time for cake."

She did it. I'm so proud of her.

She marches inside. I guess she's not going to change her mind. I follow behind. Just in time, too — a raindrop splashes on my head. I look up to see the clouds are dark again. It's going to pour.

"Time for cake," Bri calls out again.

"Bri, are you sure?" I ask, closing the door firmly behind me.

Instead of answering, she lights the candles with a shaking hand. "Everyone, let's sing!"

She's making a mistake! But what can I do? It's her mistake to make.

Everyone sings the Happy Birthday song to Jonah.

"Are we ready?" Jonah whispers to me.

"I guess so," I say.

Bri is gripping the top of a chair. Is she scared about falling asleep or nervous that she's making the wrong choice? Is she just going to conk out when Jonah blows out the candles? Is Robin going to pop up, awake? Is the portal window going to work right away? Which window will it be? Is Jonah really going to be able to fly? Or make himself invisible?

Jonah takes a big breath and blows.

All the candles go out at once. All *eleven* of them.

Here it comes. . . .

I look around.

Bri is still awake.

Jonah's not flying or invisible.

No one says anything. Everyone just stares at one another.

The room is silent.

"Nothing's happening," Jonah says at last.

The blue-haired fairy frowns. "Young man," she says. "Is it really your birthday today?"

He reddens. "Um . . ."

"It isn't, is it?"

"He doesn't look ten," another fairy whispers.

HAH!

"Birthday parties don't have to be on your birthday," Jonah grumbles. "Everyone knows that."

"Young man," Shaznay says, "when is your birthday?"

"July," Jonah replies.

Gasps echo around the room. "That's months away. You lied to us!"

"Are you even turning ten?" another fairy asks. "You're small for ten."

DOUBLE HAH!

Jonah sheepishly shakes his head.

"We do not appreciate being lied to," says the blue-haired fairy.

"We do not appreciate being used for our magic," says the teeny, tiny fairy.

"Liars don't get *wifticals*," says Shaznay.

"Noooo!" whimpers Jonah.

"But we need them," I cry.

"Tough," says the fairy on stilts. "And be warned — as Princess Brianna knows, spurned fairies often return to seek revenge."

"Please don't say that," I beg. "I don't like revenge!"

But it's too late. All of the fairies wave their wands, and with a puff of sparkle they disappear.

✳ chapter seventeen ✳

Now What?

bri is still gripping the top of the chair. "What are we supposed to do now?" she cries.

"I don't know," I say.

The sound of thunder crashes through the sky.

"I really wanted that Superpuppy," Jonah snivels.

I glance at the clock. It's already nine at night here, which means it's nine in the morning back home. Nine! How did that happen? It's so late! My parents might stroll into my room at any minute and discover we're not there. And then Robin's parents will show up and we still won't be there. My head starts to pound.

We hear a thump from upstairs.

"What is that?" Jonah asks.

I perk up. "Maybe Robin's awake?"

Bri sighs. "No. It's just Felix."

"Isn't it past his bedtime?" Jonah asks.

We hear a laugh from the attic. It's a woman's laugh. And it's not Robin's.

We all hurry up the stairs.

In the attic, the rain pummels against the skylight. Lottie and Felix are playing Karate Crocs on the floor.

"You're still here?" I ask Lottie. "I thought you left with the others."

"No. I was exploring. Felix was showing me how to do a horseyback ride. It's quite fun." She looks down at Jonah's feet. "How come you're not wearing your new socks?"

"We didn't get the *wifticals*," I admit. "It's not really Jonah's birthday. He's only seven. We're sorry."

She frowns. "You lied to me?"

We nod, ashamed.

Suddenly, the door opens and an old woman steps into the attic. Who is it? She's wrinkled and stooped over, and she's wearing a powder-blue top and matching pants. It kind of looks like a sweat suit. "Here you are," she cackles.

"Mom!" Lottie screams.

Mom? The thirteenth fairy is here? The one who cursed Bri so she would die?

She's HERE?

"Mine!" Carlotta says, and grabs the wand from Lottie's hand.

Lottie pales. "Mom, what are you doing here? I told you I'd take care of this!"

"It seems that Princess Brianna had another party and didn't invite me!" Carlotta says snidely. "How rude!"

"Mom, she invited me instead," Lottie says, biting her thumbnail. "And it wasn't a party for her this time. She didn't even create the guest list."

Bri takes a step back and glares at Carlotta. "We thought you retired." She pulls Felix behind her to protect him.

I do the same to Jonah. Carlotta may be in a sweat suit, but she's still terrifying.

"I did retire," Carlotta says, rubbing the wand against her open palm. "But even retired people come out for special occasions. And this time Bri is going to pay."

"I'm not afraid of you," Bri says, but her voice trembles.

I would be afraid of Carlotta if I was Bri. Carlotta put a death spell on Bri when she was just a baby! Is she going to try that one again? But then I realize something.

"You can't put the same spell on someone twice," I say. "It's double jeopardy!" That's a lawyerly term that means that you can't be tried for the same crime twice. I have no idea if it's true for spells. But it should be.

"Come on, Mom," Lottie says. "Haven't we done enough?"

Carlotta narrows her eyes and glares at her daughter. "While you play *games* with the prince, I'm here to give the princess what she deserves. And stop biting your nails. It's a filthy habit!"

Lottie drops her hands by her side and bows her head. She looks like she's used to hearing stuff like this.

Bri squares her shoulders. "Go ahead. Put me to sleep. I don't mind."

Carlotta cackles. "I *know* you don't mind. That's what you want! So that's not what I'm going to do. You, dear Princess, will stay awake. The rest of you, however" — she waves her wand in the air — "will sleep."

"For how long?" I ask. I have a feeling she doesn't mean a catnap.

"One hundred years," Carlotta spits out. Lightning flashes across the sky.

My heart drops to my toes. "No! We can't sleep for a hundred years. We have to go home!"

"You can't put everyone to sleep," Bri squeaks. "I'll be the only one here."

"Exactly," Carlotta says with a sly smile. "Everyone you love will wake up in the future. Your parents. Your brother. Your precious Tom. Everyone except you. By the time they wake up, you'll be dead."

Jonah grips my hand. "But we'll never see our parents again," he says.

Carlotta's eyes flash. "Tough luck for you." She waves the wand once, twice, three times in the air. Black sparkles rain down on us all. I hold my breath and brace myself for the sleep to hit.

* chapter eighteen *

Like Mother, Not Like Daughter

n o, Mom!" Lottie yells. We hear a loud *thunk*.

The black sparkles disappear into thin air.

My body sags with relief. I'm awake! We're all awake! Well, not all of us. Carlotta is crumpled on the floor.

Jonah leans toward her. "Is she breathing?"

Lottie's eyes are wide. "She's asleep. I turned the wand on her." She says the words slowly, as if she doesn't believe them herself.

"She's asleep for a hundred years?" I ask.

Lottie nods. "Or until I figure out how to wake her up."

Bri is still holding on tight to Felix. "Why did you save us?" she asks Lottie.

Lottie looks down at her mother and then back at us. "My mom was always so hard on me, you see. I wanted to be a teacher," she explains, "but my mom said I couldn't. She said I had to take over the family business." She lifts her thumbnail to her mouth to take a nibble but then shakes her head. She reaches over to the sewing contraption and gives the wheel a spin instead.

"I appreciate that you invited me even though I was so mean this morning, and even though my mom tried to . . . well, you know. Kill you." She grimaces and gives the wheel another spin. "I want to be the type of fairy that gives horseyback rides and plays Karate Crocs. Not the type of fairy who makes people die. To be honest, when I met you this morning I was planning on putting the whole palace to sleep the second you pricked your finger. I thought that would be the nice thing to do. So Bri would be with her family. I wasn't going to tell my mom, but I was going to do it. This wand may have done bad things in the past, but I'm not my mother. I'm not evil."

Aha! That's how everyone ended up asleep in the original story! Lottie felt bad for Bri!

Lottie reaches over and ruffles Felix's hair. "As a peace offering, I'll grant each of you a *wiftical*."

Yessssssss! "All five of us?" I ask eagerly.

Lottie eyes Robin. "Well, no, not the sleeping one. The four of you. Just tell me what you want."

That's an easy one. "I want Robin to wake up!"

Lottie nods. "Jonah? What do you want?"

He makes a chopping motion. "A crocodile that knows karate!"

I roll my eyes. "Jonah, come on."

He drops his hands by his sides. "I know, I know, nowhere to put it. I'll take a puppy." His eyes light up. "Superpuppy!"

I tug the sleeve of his pajama shirt. "You have to wish for a magical portal to take us home."

"But . . ." His voice trails off. "I *really* want a puppy. It doesn't even have to be Superpuppy. It can just be a regular puppy."

"No puppies! Get us home!"

He stubs his exposed toe on the floor. "I want a way for us to get home, please." He looks up at the ceiling. "Can it be the skylight? That would be so cool."

That would not be so cool. It's pouring rain. But I already feel bad about the puppy, so I keep my mouth shut.

Lottie turns to Felix. "What do you want, sweetie?"

Felix smiles. "I want a puppy!"

Jonah glares at him.

"And what about you?" Lottie asks Bri. "I guess you want to sleep for a hundred years?"

Bri looks at Felix and then at me. "I . . ." She pauses. "No."

"No?" we all repeat.

"No," she says again. "I want to stay right here."

"Since when?" I ask.

She hugs Felix even though he squirms away. "I knew for sure the moment Carlotta tried to take away my friends and family. I didn't realize what I had until it was almost gone." She shakes her head. "From now on, I'm going to appreciate what I have right in front of me. I'm going to look around and smell the roses."

I search for a rose to hand to her, but the attic seems to be the only spot in the kingdom that's rose-free. I cheer instead. "That's great, Bri! I'm so proud of you."

"Thanks," she says shyly. "Also, I realize now that I don't want to marry a prince I don't even know. I want to marry Tom."

"You do?" a voice says. We turn around. It's Tom. He has a huge smile on his face.

"I do," she replies. She takes his hand. "Tom, will you marry me?"

"I will," he says.

"I'm so happy for you guys," I cheer.

She leans over and kisses Tom on the cheek. He blushes. Hurray!

"Is there anything else you want to wish for, then?" Lottie asks Bri.

"You should wish for a bike!" Jonah says.

"Or a cell phone," I add quickly. "I'll take it if you don't want it."

Bri cocks her head to the side. "I *would* like a bike. But ever since I made those candles today, I've realized that I can make all kinds of stuff myself. Like bikes." She spins the wheel of the sewing contraption. "I've been studying this wheel, and I think I know how to make one myself."

I laugh. "You're going to invent the bicycle?"

She nods. "Yes! Exactly! Why wait a hundred years? I can invent whatever I want right now! I'm going to be an inventor!"

"You're going to be an amazing inventor," Tom says, putting his arm around her shoulders.

"So you really don't want me to wish for anything?" Lottie asks.

Bri shakes her head. "I already have everything I want right here."

"What about happiness?" Lottie asks.

Bri smiles and I can see her dimple. "I can make my own."

Jonah steps up. "Then can I please, please, pretty please with ketchup on top, use your wish to get a puppy?"

"No!" I yell. "Jonah, I would love to have a puppy, too, but we can't bring a puppy home with us!"

"Can I have a crocodile that does karate, then?" Felix asks. "Please?"

Lottie looks at Bri.

She shrugs. "Make it a teacup crocodile that does karate."

Jonah scrunches up his face. He looks like he might cry.

"Okay, then, here we go . . ." Lottie twirls her wand around and around and around. "I grant Felix one puppy and one

145

mini-crocodile that does karate. The skylight above us shall be a magical portal that goes to Smithville. And I undo the one-hundred-years sleeping curse on Robin. One. Two. Three!"

An adorable brown puppy appears and starts barking. He has floppy ears and a little black nose.

"Awwww! So cute," Jonah mumbles.

A teeny tiny green crocodile the size of my hand pops up next to Felix's foot. Its little hand goes up in what I guess is a chopping motion.

It might be small but it's still creepy.

The skylight above us starts to swirl. Yes! We have a portal!

We better not get soaked. Or hit by lightning.

"Yay! My puppy!" sings Felix. "I'm calling him Horseyback! Give me a ride, Horseyback!" Felix tries to sit on the puppy but the puppy whimpers and hides behind Jonah's leg.

And Robin . . .

Robin snores.

"Robin," I say, running over to her and taking her hands. "Robin, get up! We have to go!"

She doesn't open her eyes. "Why is she still sleeping?" I ask.

"What happened?" The skylight is swirling faster. It looks like a whirlpool.

Lottie zaps Robin again with her wand but nothing happens. "I'm sorry," she says. "I don't know why my spell didn't work. Abby, maybe you were right before when you talked about double jeopardy. A wand can't cast the same spell twice. Maybe a wand can't undo its own spell, either."

"Can you fix it?" I look up at the skylight, which is now a deep purple. "We have to go. It's really late."

"There's nothing I can do," Lottie says helplessly. "You'll have to go without her. The window will work for the next minute and then it will be gone forever."

It's already almost ten o'clock! We *have* to go. We have no choice. If Lottie can't make another portal, this is our only option. Plus, the other fairies might come back for revenge! We can't leave Robin. We'll have to take her with us.

"Maybe Maryrose will help you," Lottie says. "Her powers are much stronger than mine. Not stronger than my mom's, though."

Lottie knows Maryrose? Carlotta knows Maryrose, too? Do all the fairies know each other?

Jonah points to the skylight. "We have to go!" he cries.

"How do we get up there?" I wonder. "We usually just walk into the portal, not jump up to it!"

"What if you bounce on the bed?" Bri asks. "It's pretty springy."

"Good idea," I say. "We'll pretend it's a trampoline!"

"What's that?" Bri asks.

"Something else you should invent," I say.

Jonah and I lift Robin so that one of her arms is around my shoulders and the other is around Jonah's. Her head slumps forward but we keep her up.

"Wait!" Felix yells. He runs over to us and gives us each kisses on the cheek. Aw. We all say good-bye.

"Now jump!" I tell Jonah. We hold up Robin and jump. The puppy barks and climbs up on the bed and tries to grab Jonah's foot. We jump one more time and zoom —

The skylight sucks us right up.

✳ chapter nineteen ✳

Royal Slobber

We crash out of the mirror and land sideways on the basement floor. Me, Jonah, and a still-sleeping Robin. Ouch.

Rinnnnng!

Ack! That's the doorbell from upstairs. Robin's mom!

I look at Robin, sprawled across the floor on her back, still fast asleep. What are we going to do?

Ruff! Ruff!

I sit up, turn around, and see a small brown ball of fur.

Oh my goodness! It's the puppy! He followed us back to Smithville! We took someone home with us! Is that allowed?

"I *knew* he liked me better," Jonah says, jumping to his feet. "And I'm not naming him Horseyback. No way. What should I call him?"

The puppy sniffs Robin's hair. Then he licks her face.

"He's kissing her," Jonah says. "He's trying to wake her up."

Yes, he is kissing her.

He's kissing her.

He's KISSING her!

An idea explodes inside my head. Maybe Lottie was wrong — maybe a wand *can* undo its own spell. Maybe Lottie didn't say the RIGHT spell. Her exact words were: *I undo the one-hundred-years sleeping curse on Robin*. She undid the one-hundred-year part of the sleeping curse. But she didn't undo the part about a prince waking her up. That means that a prince can now wake her up even if a hundred years haven't passed.

"The dog's name is Prince!" I exclaim.

Jonah's eyes widen. He immediately says, "Good boy, Prince. You're such a good puppy!"

Prince the dog licks Robin's face again.

She shifts and stretches her arms above her head. She opens her eyes.

"Where am I?" she asks.

It worked! She's awake! What do I tell her? Does she remember any of it? "You're, um . . . in the basement," I say.

"I had the craziest dream," Robin says, rubbing her eyes. "We were in a tower and I pricked my elbow and then . . . I don't know. I think we were in a fairy tale. *Rapunzel*?" She rubs her elbow. "Ouch. My arm hurts." She looks around. "How did I get here?"

"You sleepwalked. There's no time to explain." I push myself off the floor. "Follow me!"

I take her by the hand and run, run, run up the stairs and to the front door.

Mom, Dad, and Robin's big sister, Dalia, are all standing in the foyer of our house. Dalia has the same curly strawberry-blonde hair as Robin, but it also has purple streaks in it. She does not look happy.

"There you are!" Mom says, turning around and sighing with relief. "We were starting to get worried. Didn't you hear us calling? You were in the basement the whole time?"

"Yes," I say, out of breath.

"All three of you?" Mom asks suspiciously.

I nod.

"Why?" Mom asks.

Think, Abby, think! "We got up really early and we were . . . um . . ."

"Robin, you're still in your pajamas!" Dalia says, putting her hands on her hips. "You better get changed fast. Mom's waiting in the car and I'm supposed to be at Tali's in five minutes. I called you a million times on your cell and you didn't answer. You have to answer your cell every time I call. Got it?"

Robin rubs her elbow. "I'm sorry, okay? I didn't hear it."

Because cell phones don't work in the Kingdom of Rose.

I think about all that happened in Rose — and about all that I learned. About how important it is to enjoy the present. To not get too caught up in the future.

Maybe I don't need to grow up *that* fast. If Bri can live in the moment, then so can I. Maybe I can wait a few years for a cell phone after all. Also, do I want my brother calling me a million times when I'm at a sleepover? No, I do not.

"You're so annoying," Dalia mutters, and Robin flushes pink.

And maybe it's not always so bad to have a younger sibling instead of an older one.

Robin runs upstairs. She hurries downstairs a minute later, her leather bag over her shoulder.

I give her a hug. "See you on Monday."

She's still rubbing her elbow. "Yeah, see you on Monday. Thank you for having me. I had a lot of fun. Next time you'll sleep at my house."

"Robin, come on!" Dalia hollers, already halfway to the car.

As I close the door behind her I take a deep breath. We did it! We got Robin home awake and in one piece!

Hurray!

"Breakfast?" Dad asks. "You must be hungry."

"Not really," Jonah says. "I had a lot of tea sandwiches."

"What, honey?" Mom asks.

I nudge my brother. "Nothing," I answer for him. We're in the clear. Let's not mess this up.

But then I hear it:

Ruff, ruff!

Oh. My. Goodness.

Dad turns toward the basement. "What was that?"

The puppy pushes open the basement door, scrambles down the hall, and jumps on Jonah's leg.

"It's Prince!" Jonah explains. "Our puppy!"

Our puppy?

HOW AM I SUPPOSED TO EXPLAIN THIS ONE?

"We have a puppy?" Mom looks incredulous.

"Er, yes," I say. Think fast! Why do we have a puppy? "We found a puppy. In the . . . um . . . backyard. Yes! The backyard! And then we . . . went to see if any of our neighbors lost a puppy. That's why we didn't hear you calling earlier. We were outside." Yes! That makes sense. Maybe not perfect sense, but a little bit of sense. Right?

My parents are looking at us suspiciously.

"Jonah went outside in his pajamas with no shoes?" Mom asks. "And, Abby — what are you wearing? Where did you get that outfit?"

Oops. I'm still in Bri's blue dress. "Um, it's Robin's. She loaned it to me. I'll bring it back to her at school on Monday."

Mom frowns. I'm not sure she believes me at all. "Okay," she says finally. "But be careful with it. It looks expensive."

Jonah scoops up the puppy and lets it lick his face. "Can we keep the puppy?" Jonah asks. His face is pleading. "Pretty please? We named him Prince. Isn't he cute?" Jonah hands him to Dad, and Prince licks Dad's face.

My dad laughs. "He's very energetic."

"I don't know about this," Mom says.

"Please, please, please?" Jonah asks.

Mom opens her mouth but then closes it. Is she softening? I think she is. She looks at Dad and shrugs.

No way. My heart leaps. Is she actually considering letting us keep the puppy?

"We'll take care of him!" I squeal. "I'll walk him every day!"

Jonah jumps on his toes. "I'll feed him! Good stuff, too, not just ketchup!"

Mom and Dad eye each other over the fur.

"It could be fun. . . ." Mom says.

"It would teach them responsibility. . . ." Dad adds.

I hold my breath.

"All right," Mom says finally. "We'll have to try and find the original owners first, but if we can't . . ."

"We can keep him?" Jonah asks.

"You can keep him," my mom says. "But honestly, kids, don't get too attached yet, in case we have to give him back." She ruffles his fur. "Who's a cutie?" she asks in baby talk.

Jonah and I give each other a knowing smile.

Smithville finally has its own prince.

"I'm going to take a nap," I announce after lunch. I can barely keep my eyes open. I have major fairy tale jet lag.

"Good idea," Mom says. "I bet you girls were up all night chatting."

Not exactly. But I nod and head upstairs. Prince follows right behind me. What a sweetie. He's like a real live teddy bear.

I'm about to get into bed when I remember to check my jewelry box. I spot the image of Bri right away. Instead of lying asleep on the bed, she's riding a bicycle . . . and smiling.

I smile, too. I climb under my covers. Prince jumps on my bed and smushes his little body against mine.

I can't believe we brought a puppy back with us.

Sure, we've brought stuff back before — clothes and shoes and such — but never something LIVING.

I stroke my fingers over his fur. If Prince can come back — does that mean other characters can come back, too?

Maybe Bri or one of the other princesses could come visit!

Although if one of the princesses could come, that means one of the not-so-nice people could come visit, too. Like Carlotta.

I shudder. I don't even want to think about what could happen then.

Prince buries his nose in the mattress and closes his eyes.

"Tired?" I ask between yawns.

He yawns back. Yawns really are contagious.

"Should we take a little nap?"

I'll worry about Carlotta or other evil characters coming to Smithville later. Now, I close my eyes, lay my hand on Prince's back, and murmur, "Sweet dreams."

Don't miss Abby and Jonah's next adventure,
where they meet Rapunzel!

Look for:

Whatever After #5: BAD HAIR DAY

acknowledgments

Thank you, thank you, thank you to: Laura Dail, Tamar Rydzinski, Aimee Friedman (world's fastest and most responsive editor!), Abby McAden, David Levithan, Becky Shapiro, Becky Amsel, Bess Braswell, Allison Singer, Janet Robbins, Lizette Serrano, Emily Sharpe, Emily Heddleson, Candace Greene, AnnMarie Anderson, Courtney Sheinmel, Emily Bender, Anne Heltzel, Lauren Myracle, E. Lockhart (double thanks for your awesome notes!), Tori, Carly and Carol Adams, Targia Alphonse, Shaznay Calixte (who has a great name!), Jess Braun, Lauren Kisilevsky, Bonnie Altro, Susan Finkelberg-Sohmer, Corinne and Michael Bilerman, Jess Rothenberg, Adele Griffin, Leslie Margolis, Robin Wasserman, Maryrose Wood, Tara Altebrando, Sara Zarr, Ally Carter, Jennifer Barnes, Alan Gratz, Penny Fransblow, Maggie Marr, and Farrin Jacobs.

Love and thanks to my family: Aviva, Dad, Louisa, Mom, Robert, Gary, Lori, Sloane, Isaac, Vickie, John, Gary, Darren, Ryan, Jack, Jen, Teri, Briana, Michael, David, Patsy, Murray, Maggie, and Jenny.

Extra love and thanks to my husband, Todd.

Hello, Chloe Michelle Swidler. I love you. I know you want to see your full name in a book, so here it is! To avoid sibling rivalry: Anabelle Morgan Swidler, I love you, too. Thank you both for being so smart and sweet even though you didn't have a *wiftical* party. Or maybe you did. . . .

Each time Abby and Jonah get sucked into
their magic mirror, they wind up in a different
fairy tale — and find new adventures!

Turn the page to read all about the
Whatever After series!

Whatever After #1: FAIREST of ALL

In their first adventure, Abby and Jonah wind up in the story of Snow White. But when they stop Snow from eating the poisoned apple, they realize they've messed up the whole story! Can they fix it — and still find Snow her happy ending?

Whatever After #2: IF the SHOE FITS

This time, Abby and Jonah find themselves in Cinderella's story. When Cinderella breaks her foot, the glass slipper won't fit! With a little bit of magic, quick thinking, and luck, can Abby and her brother save the day?

Whatever After #3: SINK or SWIM

Abby and Jonah are pulled into the tale of the Little Mermaid —
a story with an ending that is *not* happy. So Abby and Jonah mess
it up on purpose! Can they convince the mermaid to keep her tail
before it's too late?

. . . And more stories to come!

Sarah Mlynowski is the author of the Magic in Manhattan series, *Gimme a Call*, and a bunch of other books for tweens and teens. Originally from Montreal, Sarah now lives in the kingdom of Manhattan with her very own prince charming and their fairy-tale-loving daughters. Visit Sarah online at www.sarahm.com.

Author photo by Sigrid Estrada